SPECIAL MESSAGE TO READERS

This book is published under the auspices of

THE ULVERSCROFT FOUNDATION

(registered charity No. 264873 UK)

Established in 1972 to provide funds for research, diagnosis and treatment of eye diseases. Examples of contributions made are: —

A Children's Assessment Unit at Moorfield's Hospital, London.

•

Twin operating theatres at the Western Ophthalmic Hospital, London.

•

A Chair of Ophthalmology at the Royal Australian College of Ophthalmologists.

•

The Ulverscroft Children's Eye Unit at the Great Ormond Street Hospital For Sick Children, London.

You can help further the work of the Foundation by making a donation or leaving a legacy. Every contribution, no matter how small, is received with gratitude. Please write for details to:

THE ULVERSCROFT FOUNDATION,
The Green, Bradgate Road, Anstey,
Leicester LE7 7FU, England.
Telephone: (0116) 236 4325

In Australia write to:
THE ULVERSCROFT FOUNDATION,
c/o The Royal Australian College of
Ophthalmologists,
27, Commonwealth Street, Sydney,
N.S.W. 2010.

Lynn Nixon was born in 1945 and is a retired Chief Inspector of police. During her police career she served in many locations throughout the UK. She now resides in Dunoon, Scotland with her husband Joe, a retired Detective Chief Inspector. She has four stepchildren and a grandson to date. Originally a 'Geordie', Lynn married Joe, as he says, 'to avoid her being a stateless person, as Geordies are neither Scots nor English'; a comment that has given rise to much discussion in the household. Lynn now enjoys, with a little help from Joe, writing detective novels using their vast police experience.

DEATH OF A REVEREND GENTLEMAN

The headless body of Reverend Campbell is found within the kirk grounds in Kilmun, a small village on the west coast of Scotland, the day before he was due to move. So for Detective Chief Inspector MacLeod there begins an intriguing investigation which, ironically, shows that the Reverend was no gentleman and far from worthy of reverence.

LYNN NIXON

DEATH OF A REVEREND GENTLEMAN

Complete and Unabridged

WARWICKSHIRE
COUNTY LIBRARY

CONTROL No.

ULVERSCROFT
Leicester

First published in Great Britain in 1998 by
Citron Press
London

First Large Print Edition
published 2000
by arrangement with
Citron Press Limited
London

This book is a work of fiction. Names, characters, places and incidents are either products of the author's imagination or are used fictitiously. Any resemblance to actual events or locales or persons, living or dead, is entirely coincidental.

Copyright © 1998 by Lynn Nixon
All rights reserved

British Library CIP Data

Nixon, Lynn
    Death of a reverend gentleman.
    —Large print ed.—
    Ulverscroft large print series: mystery
    1. Detective and mystery stories
    2. Large type books
    I. Title
    823.9′14 [F]

    ISBN 0–7089–4321–7

Published by
F. A. Thorpe (Publishing)
Anstey, Leicestershire
Set by Words & Graphics Ltd.
Anstey, Leicestershire
Printed and bound in Great Britain by
T. J. International Ltd., Padstow, Cornwall

This book is printed on acid-free paper

1

'Enough! This jealousy is driving me crazy.'
The Reverend William Campbell stood at the
door of the Manse; he held the doorknob in
a grip so hard his knuckles were white. His
wife Julia looked at him accusingly from the
living room door. Packing cases filled the hall
and were a physical barrier, mimicking the
mental barrier between them.

'I think I have reason, don't you?' Julia
appeared calm. Inside she was angry, upset,
jealous and frightened, a turmoil of emotions
she simply couldn't control. It was a regular
and sad argument, but usually one sided.
William rarely raised his voice but this time
she sensed emotion in his words, emotion she
was hoping would end in a reunion. They
lived in the same house but they were never
together, either physically or emotionally.

'I do not think you have reason Julia, I will
come back when you have calmed down.' He
almost spat the words out; each was a bullet
flying towards her, which found their mark.
He left slamming the oak door behind him,
the sound echoed throughout the house.

Julia crumpled and sat down on the stairs.

She put her head in her hands and allowed a few tears to flow down her face. She hated herself for starting the row, but she loved him so much. If only he would move back into her bed, then she could at least hold him in her arms and try to make things better. He had moved into the 'spare room' some fifteen years previously without any explanation and no amount of questioning on her part could elicit the reason for his callous abandonment of her. William always locked the door and she couldn't even join him.

As a full-blooded woman she missed their lovemaking and occasionally thought about having an affair, but her upbringing precluded that course of action. If only he would explain what she had done — or not done — or what had happened. One day he was there, the next gone. If he had left her it would have been kinder. She could have started again, once the pain had gone, but this was half living, a sham, and a pale shadow of life.

She knew that William had other women, too many for her to count. She could always tell when someone new came into his life. She wouldn't know her name but he developed new mannerisms, new words here or a gesture there. Perhaps it was the way he ate, or used an unfamiliar phrase, but she knew. He was a serial lover. She would have been better off if he had been a serial killer; at least she would have known where he was — in prison, behind bars.

She sat on the stairs with her knees pulled up to her chest, her arms clasped tight around her legs, her grey skirt crumpled tightly. She sat for a few minutes then sighed; this was getting her nowhere, and she gazed around the hallway and decided to carry on packing their belongings. She stood up and pulled the collar of her white blouse straight; she tutted when she saw a smudge on the sleeve, having only put it on clean this morning. She never wore make-up except a lick of eye shadow and lipstick, so it had to be the dust from packing. No matter, she would change tomorrow. In any case William never noticed what she wore and she was not going to cause more washing now.

Mentally and physically she shrugged her shoulders, and wished she could do the same for her marriage, but unfortunately the vows she had taken at her wedding were imprinted in her mind. For richer or poorer, in sickness and in health, there's no mention of what to do when the 'love' disappeared, and having taken the old vows of 'honour and obey', her sense of duty was too strong to break the solemn covenant with God.

Julia wished she had been brought up in

the modern open-minded generation where casting off marriage and taking another seemed to be the same as casting off clothes. She was as parsimonious with her clothing as she was with her marriage. Julia did not discard anything unless it was completely worn out and even then she used the clothing as dusters and dishcloths. Her mother had taught her well.

As the wife of a minister the care she took over the pennies was necessary. A minister would never be rich and she ensured that they would at least keep out of debt. 'God,' she said in silent conversation to her Maker, 'I want a normal marriage so please bring him back to me. My mother told me that there is no greater hell on earth than an unhappy marriage and *she was right*. I don't want anyone else and I don't want him to die but if it is the only way, can you do something about it?' Julia was shocked at the thought that she had asked God to get her husband permanently out of the way, and made an extra prayer: 'I didn't really mean he should die, I just want him back.'

She looked around the hallway; the boxes packed, but yet to be sealed, with the accumulation of goods over a lifetime of marriage, did not amount to much. They had little furniture that they could call their

4

own. The Manse was usually fully furnished when they took over the living and all they needed was linen, crockery and knick-knacks to make it a home rather than a house.

Julia was not a person who could walk into a house and set things down to make it into a beautiful place. She didn't have the flair and she was jealous of those who did. She was not a homebody as such, and no matter how many magazines she read and whose ideas she tried to copy, somehow it just didn't work.

Julia sighed and got up; she would have to get the rest of the things in their boxes. The recent argument with William receded into the background. They had been at each other's throats so many times over the years, the arguments had become some sort of ritual. When she burst into tears it was a signal that the fleeting emotional outburst was over and they would go back to being studiously polite to each other, giving the appearance of a solid marriage for the benefit of the community which William served. It was not good for a minister to have an unhappy marriage; the minds of the parishioners should be on the word of God, not the word of rumour and whispers of their spiritual leader's antics.

5

The wind pressed against William and he huddled against the onslaught. With an effort he walked up the steep steps to the prettiest church he had ever had the pleasure of working in. It was silhouetted against the skyline on the top of a small hill overlooking the Clyde estuary, surrounded by the ancient graveyard of generations of residents. The graveyard held the remains of at least one famous person, Elizabeth Blackwell, the first women to become a doctor. She had not been the first female to qualify fully as a doctor; another could claim that right but that other woman had disguised her sex to enter the bastion of a male preserve. Elizabeth had been accepted as a student without such subterfuge and graduated. She had done so in America; it was many years before the barriers were to come down in this country.

William had no thoughts of Elizabeth Blackwell in his mind at the moment; he had his own strong woman at home and did not wish to dwell on another. He was feeling content and was looking forward to moving to Oban; although in his own mind he thought of this kirk as his real home.

In fact, the affinity he felt was emotional

rather than real, probably due to the fact that this was the last resting-place of his clan chiefs, the Campbells. The mausoleum at the back of the kirk was the last resting-place of the Clan Chiefs dating from the fifteenth century. He knew he would never have the privilege of being interred there; he held the name Campbell, but was too far down in the hierarchy to aspire to such an honour, however he felt he had given something to this wonderful community in the name of the Campbells.

Kilmun is a small and largely unknown part of the west coast of Scotland, lying some five miles from the town of Dunoon. It is a lovely village built on the slopes along the shoreline of Holy Loch, the mostly granite houses clinging to the hill and loch side. There is a golf course, but it is not for the faint-hearted. To accommodate the enthusiastic sportsmen, trees on one side of the hill have been cleared, on the flattest place possible. It is only a nine-hole course but is known locally as Cardiac Hill; there is no plush nineteenth hole, unlike the courses in Dunoon or Largs, definitely not; there is a small hut with an honesty box for payment for a round of golf. Some tired and exhausted golfers have been known to whisper that they should be paid to play the course, not the other way round. Kilmun is not on the tourist route as such, but loved by the people who live there. William was no different.

When William reached the porch of the kirk he straightened up to his full height, and shook his greying hair, longer than would be expected of a minister. It was his only vanity and he looked forward to the day when it would be completely white rather than the pepper and salt of middle age. He had always admired snow-white hair and he knew he would not go bald; his father had kept his hair all his life. All the Campbell men had a good mane; he was fortunate that his genetic make-up avoided the trials of other men who grieved for the loss of their crowning glories.

William was a tall man of fifty and time had been kind to him. As a youth he had been gangly with an unfair share of acne. With age he had filled out and his pockmarked skin gave him a craggy rather than ravaged look. The dark, heavy-rimmed spectacles that he wore enhanced his appearance and gave him an air of gravity and trustworthiness.

It was late on the Saturday evening when William arrived at the kirk and pushed the heavy doors open. It was not a modern kirk, but a religious site from the mists of time, and Christianity had happily taken it over; after all the early Christians were nothing but opportunists. From antiquity each generation had added its own buildings and identity, until the present kirk appeared, having been built in the late nineteenth century. A solid edifice of the Victorian era for those who cared deeply about the hereafter and their own souls in particular.

The only additions since then had been the more modern heating and lighting systems. To stop the bells shaking the building to its foundations a modern loudspeaker was used with a peal of bells on tape, not in keeping with the building perhaps, but it saved a great deal of expensive maintenance. The real bells can be heard on special occasions, to William's anxious prayers that no more of the building should be shaken loose and hopefully no-one should be hurt. The restoration fund was always grateful for the proceeds of car boot sales, fetes and the sale of teas to visitors.

It was William's usual practice to spend some time alone in the kirk when he had an important service the following day. Tomorrow was such a day; it was his last service in the kirk he loved. His choice of time depended on the activities. Saturday evening

9

was seldom busy now. When the kirk was the centre of communal activities, the hall was often used for highland dancing and Scottish musical evenings and dances, even pie 'n' pea suppers. The advent of television and other more attractive forms of entertainment had made the organised kirk functions die a slow and uncomplaining death.

It was twilight and William decided not to turn on the lights, there was enough muted light silently streaming through the stained glass to guide his way. 'The last time,' he thought, 'off to Oban on Monday. I will miss the old place'.

He touched the cold stones and felt there was a vibrancy of joy. He felt he was communing with his predecessors and took in a deep breath, the ice-cold air that flowed into his lungs was tinged with a faint smell of dying flowers. The smell reminded him of his argument with Julia earlier, she wore flowery perfume that physically repelled him — in fact *she* physically repelled him. Sometime after the first years of marriage something had happened, he was at a loss to say what or when, but he found her close proximity unbearable. That was his reason for moving into the spare room, but he could not tell her. She was the mother of his children and he could not abandon her.

He had hoped she might leave him. As a minister he could not leave her and remain in the Church. He persevered in controlling his repulsion and eventually found his life tolerable, and carried on as best he could. The children were now grownup and perhaps he could think of changing, more for Julia's sake, or perhaps he should admit that it was for his own sake, he would have to give up his work if he left her. The Church of Scotland did not approve of divorce within their own Ministry and definitely did not approve of adultery. He would wait and see what the future brought. He *had* to do something and soon, Julia would forget him in time and she was a handsome woman. She would soon find another partner who would give her what he could not. This was not the time or place to think of these things, he had to settle himself down and get on with the most important reason he was here, giving thanks to God for his life in Kilmun and asking for guidance for the future.

William had been happy with his life here, but always the pragmatist, he looked forward to his new post in Oban, it was a bigger community. He knew he would be happy no matter where he was, as long as he could follow his vocation.

Kilmun was a small but God-fearing community on the west coast of Scotland. Although not as 'Christian' as the Shetlands or Hebrides, where most shops closed on the Lord's day, there was still a streak of ingrained righteous morality and most people attended their particular church on a regular basis. The peace of this kirk permeated into his soul and settled him down after the recent argument with his wife.

William walked down the aisle towards the altar and suddenly became aware that he was not alone. He felt the presence of another person but he could not see anyone. He peered into the gloom and looked for the person he knew was there. He heard breathing from the small corridor towards the vestry. William felt no fear, this was not a ghostly apparition he heard, in fact he had never felt the presence of earthbound spirits in the kirk, although there was supposed to be at least one lonely stranger mournfully haunting the buildings.

The local community used this holy place in times of trial and also in times of great joy. It was not strange to William that when things are plodding along nicely God is forgotten. Now it was visited mainly by tourists who had made the effort to see a historical kirk. But not usually so late in the evening.

'Who's there?' he called. 'Come, we can pray together.' A figure appeared from the shadows and William smiled. It was his last smile.

2

Mrs Grace Jones woke early on Sunday; the storm of the previous night had abated to reveal a glorious summer morning. She remembered that it was her turn to arrange the flowers in the church and should have done it the previous evening. She lived a mere five hundred yards away from the church but the weather last night had forced her to stay indoors. Grace didn't have a car since she and her husband had divorced some years earlier and either walked or rode her bicycle to get to work and do the local shopping. Having a car wouldn't have done anything to help her stay dry last night, for the walk up the steep steps to the kirk door was open to the elements and any attempt to use an umbrella in that storm would have been futile.

Grace worked as a receptionist at the local health centre, for two doctors who were, she felt, in her charge. She looked after them with pride, but was not the 'ogre' of the desk. Grace knew when someone was genuinely ill and when it was a 'swing the lead, I want a day off to go to the

14

football' person. So did her employers and they trusted her judgement to some extent. She erred on the side of caution and often let the 'lead swingers' through, much to her disgust when she found out later how she had been misled.

Although in her early forties, Grace had married young and her children were now grown up. Her daughter, Shona, had married at eighteen. 'Far too young,' she had told her, but as she herself had married at seventeen, and had given birth to Shona at eighteen, there was little room to be critical. Ewen, her son, had gone to University two years ago and apart from a few hectic visits she rarely saw either of them.

As Grace hurried to the church, she felt a slight chill in the air and pulled her woollen coat tightly around her trim figure. She pulled a headscarf from her pocket and put it on; old habits die hard, for she felt it was somehow blasphemous to enter the Lord's house with her auburn hair uncovered. Grace never wore a hat, or covered her hair, even in the wildest of weather, except in the Lord's House; she had seen too many retired ladies and ladies of her own age who would not dream of going anywhere without a hat. Grace wondered sometimes whether they actually went to bed with their hats on their

15

head. She had come to believe that old age equated to hats and vowed not to become part of that generation, feeling herself young in spirit and always wishing to remain so.

Grace's heart was light today, she had no worries and was looking forward to a pleasant Sunday once her duty had been done. There were to be no visitors, and she had decided to make herself her favourite meal, stovies, a real Scottish delicacy in her opinion. Potatoes, corned beef, onion and carrot mashed together into a mountain onto a plate, smothered in butter and perhaps tomato sauce, a real comfort food and not for anyone on a diet; in Grace's opinion real food is rarely for those watching their figures.

New flowers had been delivered to the kirk yesterday morning from the local florist, and Grace enjoyed making an elegant display. The admiring looks from her fellow volunteer ladies in the kirk always pleased her; she knew it was a small sin, but one that the Lord would overlook.

As she was tying the headscarf, she glanced over to the graveyard. She stopped in her tracks; she felt her breath stop and her stomach heave. There, lying on the flat stone of a grave, was a body. She could clearly see that the head was missing. The body was clothed in a black coat, and even from this distance she could see it was lying on its back and appeared to be male. Its arms were spread wide; a large knife had been driven through the stomach.

Grace felt her knees buckle and the bile rise in her throat; she gulped and mentally took hold of herself. She felt as if she were about to faint, but forced her legs to move and walked unsteadily back towards the gate. As much as she wanted to run, her legs had a mind of their own and it felt like hours before she got to the safety of the outer gate.

She leant on the cold stones of the church wall and felt a little strength return to her body. She took a deep breath and was about to go further when she heard a familiar and welcome voice.

'Hi, Mum, I thought you would be here.' It was her son Ewen. He was a tall gangly youth with a dazzling smile, too much like his father for Grace's liking, but he was her baby and she loved him as only a mother can for the youngest in the family. Ewen was slightly out of breath, he had run up the steps from the road and his face was flushed. As he neared her he saw her ashen face and his sunny smile became full of concern.

'What on earth is the matter?' Ewen asked.

Grace sagged into his arms, her head resting on his chest. Ewen put his arms around her to stop her falling and clutched her tightly when she said 'Get the police, there's been a murder.'

Ewen physically held her up and said, 'Come with me, you need to lie down.'

'No.' She straightened up and pushed him away from her. 'Go and ring the police, I'll stay here and stop anyone else seeing . . . ' Her voice trailed off. She gave him an encouraging shove in the chest and he reluctantly walked away. He took two steps towards their home and suddenly turned and went towards the entrance of the churchyard.

'No! No!' Grace shouted and grabbed his arm; she yanked him away and he almost fell onto the gravel path. 'Don't go in there.' She desperately wanted to shield her son from the horror. 'Go home and ring the police.' She pulled him upright and propelled him towards the cottage.

He ruefully rubbed his arm and looked at his mother. She had rarely been so harsh with him. 'She must really mean it,' he thought. As he turned to go she said to him, 'Anyway, what are you doing here? I thought you were in Glasgow.'

Ewen replied over his shoulder as he began

18

to run towards the house, 'I went to a party in Dunoon last night and we were thrown out this morning, so I thought I would come home and get some rest.'

'Some party!' she thought, but she was grateful that at least he was here today. She knew she needed him. Her thoughts returned to the 'thing' lying on the gravestone. 'Hurry son,' Grace urged Ewen, 'get the police as fast as you can.' She took a deep breath and became stronger by the minute. Ewen's presence helped.

'Some rest I'm going to get this weekend,' Ewen thought ruefully as he ran home.

★ ★ ★

Sergeant Gillespie was sitting comfortably in his office at Dunoon police station contemplating a quiet Sunday. He loved working in this area, although he found that he was understaffed at times, and this was one of those times. He had two officers to cover the whole of the area and one to man the office, but he knew that most people were law-abiding citizens and Sundays were usually peaceful. The troublemakers of the previous evening had slept it off in the cells and he had thrown them out about forty-five minutes earlier.

These students were a trial at times, going off to University then coming home at weekends to blow off steam. He wished they would stay in Glasgow, Stirling or Edinburgh, anywhere but come home to party. Fifteen years was a long time on the Cowal Peninsular; mostly officers were moved on regularly. Sergeant Gillespie had thought about the question often, he sometimes had an urge to ask why he had been left alone so long but changed his mind. Once the 'Administrators' recognised his existence they would most certainly move him on. 'No,' he thought, 'best not remind them I exist, whilst they have forgotten about me I'll be fine. Just keep my head down for now, I'll ask when I really want to move'.

The phone rang; it was a breathless Ewen Jones who gave him the worst of news. 'There's been a murder, Mum told me to get you quick.'

Sergeant Gillespie immediately thought that the call might be a hoax. He hoped it was. Ewen was one of the students he had ejected earlier with a flea in his ear, but he could not quite believe he would be so foolish as to perpetrate a hoax so soon after he had been in custody. He said, 'Ewen, this is not funny, I hope you are joking.'

'No, sorry, it's real I'm afraid,' said Ewen,

slightly affronted that Sergeant Gillespie would think he could be so stupid.

'All right, tell me what happened,' asked Sergeant Gillespie.

'I don't know, Mum wouldn't let me see the body, but it must be odd or she wouldn't have told me to call you. It's at the kirk. Oh, and Sergeant, please don't say anything to Mum about last night, she has enough on her mind.' The voice sounded hopeful.

'I'll think about that, now get back to her, but don't touch anything and stop anyone else getting near the body.' He thought, 'Ewen is a nice boy, but easily led by others. I won't tell his mum but I'll let him sweat a little.'

Sergeant Gillespie sighed; he prayed it was not murder and that death was by natural causes, he didn't have enough staff to cope with anything else. As he passed the office he said to Constable Anderson, 'Where are the other two?' He was dismayed to learn that they had gone to Otter Ferry, some fifteen miles away. 'Get them back, and tell them to meet me at Kilmun church and don't leave the office for a moment. I'll be calling in soon. Ewen Jones has reported a murder,' he said as he left the police station.

Constable Anderson had been reading the Sunday papers when Sergeant Gillespie came out of his office at a fast rate of knots. He was a young constable hardly out of his probationary period, just at the stage in his career when he knew enough to know it all, and too little to know that he knew nothing. He had never been 'involved' with a crime such as this and all the training he had been given seemed to zoom out of the window. He became what he was; a young man lacking confidence often hiding behind the uniform he wore. Unfortunately his lack of confidence came out as arrogance and he offended many members of the public with his manner. He would learn slowly and really become a useful member of the force, or he would make a gigantic mistake and be thrown out. There can be no middle way with 'uniform carriers.'

He flung the newspaper to the ground and began to shout into the radio, calling his colleagues. There was panic in his voice and Sergeant Gillespie overheard the jabbering of a young man in fear. He was about to interrupt the call when he changed his mind; there would be time later to sort him out. 'Oh why do I always get the hard ones to train?' he thought.

Sergeant Gillespie arrived at the church at the same time as some parishioners who were arriving to attend early morning service. Mrs

Jones was at the church gate stopping anyone from entering. He overheard her say to Mrs Helen MacDonald, the local news reporter, 'I don't care who you are, it isn't right, it isn't decent and it's horrible.'

It looked as though Mrs MacDonald, known to the local police as 'The Wicked Witch of the West', a much bigger and stronger woman than Mrs Jones, was about to physically push her aside when Sergeant Gillespie shouted, 'Helen, stay where you are. Show some respect for the deceased.'

Helen MacDonald turned to Sergeant Gillespie, 'Oh, it's you, Sergeant, I wasn't going anywhere.' She gave a nervous giggle and stepped back to allow him to pass.

'Helen, take over from Mrs Jones and stop anyone else from coming in,' he said and turned to Grace Jones. 'Show me where the body is.'

'No,' Grace said with a slight edge of hysteria in her voice, 'I'm not going back, no, no, no.'

Sergeant Gillespie held her hands gently and said, 'All right, but tell me where it is.'

'You can't miss it, it's on the grave next to the porch,' said Grace Jones, her voice calming down a little when she realised that she would not have to go back to that place, though her appearance gave every sign that she was on the verge of collapse.

'Where's Ewen?' Sergeant Gillespie asked.

'I sent him home,' said Grace. 'He wanted to see the body and I wouldn't let him so I sent him home to have a lie down. He was at a party last night and I expect he's very tired.'

Sergeant Gillespie smiled. He could have told Grace that her son had plenty of sleep in the cells, but she had enough on her plate without her knowing where her son had been during the night. She was a proud woman and the knowledge that her son had spent the night in prison bringing shame on the family could possibly cause a real breakdown. He would have to tell her sometime, but now was not the time.

Sergeant Gillespie turned to Helen MacDonald and said, 'Helen, I really mean it, no-one is to come in without my say so, and that includes you. Do you understand?' He said to Grace, 'Will you wait here until I get back, it won't take long, Helen will keep you company.' He looked at Helen who nodded in agreement.

Helen saw how frightened Grace was and in need of her support. She decided that if she played her cards right and did what Sergeant Gillespie wanted she could have an exclusive interview. As always she was the professional reporter and looked to the future, although she was more upset than she would admit. She hated murders — there was always more than one victim. The families rarely got over such a heinous crime, both the victim's and the perpetrator's, not forgetting friends on both sides of the camp.

Sergeant Gillespie walked slowly towards the place indicated by Grace Jones and took in the scene immediately; he saw a body lying on the gravestone and shuddered, there didn't appear to be a head. As he approached he saw a mass of congealed blood where the head should have been. He carefully walked to where the body was in full view in order not to disturb any possible forensic clues. Gillespie was horrified; this was an abomination, a blasphemy, and a horror. He saw a male body, clad in a black overcoat. Although there was no head, Gillespie had a strong and overwhelming recognition that this was The Reverend William Campbell. He couldn't stay any longer and ran back to the comforting presence of other live human beings.

As he reached the gate he mentally took hold of himself and forced himself to slow down to a walk. Helen and Grace looked at him with concern. He was ashen faced.

'You look unwell, Sergeant,' said Helen, 'is there anything I can do?'

'Yes, you can help by making sure that no-one, and I mean no-one, goes into the churchyard.' He said it with both emphasis and a pleading at the same time.

Helen was a little startled. 'He really does need me,' she thought with some sense of satisfaction. This was the first time he had ever, and she meant *ever*, asked her for help and meant it. Sergeant Gillespie had been a worthy adversary and seeing how shaken he was showed another side of his character, one Helen quite liked. It was the first time he had appeared vulnerable. 'So there is a real man under that alligator hide.' She eyed him with interest and decided to try to take advantage of this sudden vulnerability.

'You can depend on me but I want an exclusive from you.'

'I'll see what I can do.' Gillespie made a foolish half promise he would later regret. He put his moment of weakness down to shock when she eventually came back to him.

'Do you know who it is?' asked Grace. An image of a bloodstained white collar swam into view and Sergeant Gillespie leant on the wall for support. 'Has anyone seen the Reverend Campbell this morning?' he asked. Grace fainted.

3

Detective Chief Inspector MacLeod was up early; he was reading his newspaper and having a nice cup of tea. It was a glorious Sunday morning, the sun was shining and all was right with the world. His wife was having a lie in and his two daughters Jacqueline and Nicola would not surface for hours yet.

Teenage years are trying for both children and parents but the only saving grace for MacLeod was that they stayed in bed until noon or even later at weekends. Thus the arguments and spats with each other and their parents are limited to those hours when they are actually awake, or what passes for consciousness, whilst their hormones are rampant. It was so peaceful whilst they slept. MacLeod hated uproar in the house, at times he longed for the days when the girls were younger and the world was fresh and new to them. World-weary teenagers were not something he could cope with and he much appreciated the calm times when they were out or asleep. MacLeod loved his children dearly but looked forward to the day when the girls would grow up and at least become friends. The constant bickering gave him indigestion; he hated arguments at home. He had enough friction at work, but recently he was finding it all too much.

Morag his wife seemed to cope well and kept telling him that they were only children and somewhere in the sulky teenagers they had become was his sunny disposition so they would grow out of it. It was only a phase in life. MacLeod was inordinately proud of his children. They would do well in life, no matter what they did and he would support them as far as he could, and he knew they had been given a good upbringing to stay on the right side of the law.

MacLeod could not keep his eye on them all the time and he knew of respectable families torn apart by watching their intelligent and beautiful children degenerate into drugs or crime. Should that happen to his girls he suspected he would do something violent to whomsoever it was who dragged them in that direction.

Perhaps the training he received in the Army was overriding his police training where his family was concerned. Sometimes he had a conflict in his soul, being trained to kill as a young man and then being trained to save lives was the cause of his contradictory behaviour. Most of his supervisors had never seen a drill square and the menace he showed at times made them wary of him. MacLeod was known as a man not to cross. If he was angry he became very quiet which was unnerving to the bravest of his colleagues.

MacLeod was about to take a refill of tea when the phone rang. He rushed into the hallway to stop its urgent ring before it disturbed Morag, but he was too late for that. As he answered the phone he saw her at the top of the stairs in her dressing gown, sleepily rubbing her eyes. She heard him say, 'Keep the area sterile, Sergeant Gillespie. Get my team together and I'll be there as soon as possible.'

MacLeod looked up at his wife and shrugged his shoulders. Morag had the light of the hall window behind her and he thought how lucky he was, she had kept the girlish figure she had when they had first married and her startling blue eyes had not dimmed through the years. Morag turned without a word and went into their bedroom.

MacLeod walked quietly up the stairs; he now had the desire to awaken his children, and saw his wife getting out his overnight bag from the wardrobe. He went over and kissed her on the forehead, 'Sorry, but I've got to go.'

Morag shrugged and said, 'I know.'

'How do you know I'll need my over-nighter?' he asked.

'Don't be silly, Sergeant Gillespie is in Dunoon. You would have told me if he had been moved. He's almost a fixture there like Highland Mary's Statue, so you will need your bag, at least two nights' worth I believe.' Morag was practical where Cameron's work was concerned. She felt no animosity that their weekend had been so rudely interrupted. She was married to a policeman and however much she resented the intrusion of 'the Job' into their private lives, she was too much in love and proud of her husband to ever give him cause for concern. He had his job to do and that was that. She was quite capable of running the home and looking after the domestic matters so that he was free to get on with his work. Morag had lost count of the times he had missed birthdays and wedding anniversaries because of his work. She would always give him her wholehearted support, though sometimes she looked forward to his retirement with a sense of longing.

★ ★ ★

MacLeod raced his old car through Gourock towards the Western Ferry terminal at

30

McInroys Point. He hoped the young men of the local police were occupied elsewhere. If they were out and about, he would pay a heavy fine for speeding. They loved to catch police officers, especially senior police officers. If he missed this ferry he had half an hour to wait for the next. The ferry was in the docking bay as he screeched into the car park. They were about to cast off but saw MacLeod coming and waved him on. Unlike other forms of public transport the ferry master would wait a couple of minutes for latecomers, he took no pleasure in leaving customers behind.

MacLeod settled down and the ticket collector, young Robert, knocked on the window. 'Hello Mr MacLeod, going to Kilmun to see about the body are you?'

MacLeod's mouth opened in shock. 'How do you know?' After all he had been told only a matter of twenty minutes earlier.

'It's gone round, one of my last passengers told me,' Robert replied. 'You know that nothing happens here without everyone knowing. You are a Dunoon man after all, even though you 'emigrated' to the other side.'

MacLeod smiled. One and a half miles of water separated Dunoon from the 'mainland' but there was a difference in both lifestyle and thinking. Neither was better or worse than the other, but one was slower and more genteel. It didn't take a genius to guess which was slower, it wasn't inferior, just different. After all Greenock had the rare distinction of having arrived. There was actually a 'drive-thru' Macdonald's on the main road into town. Dunoon would never be able to boast such decadence; the population was just too small to support such an enterprise.

'Well as you seem to know more about this than I do, you couldn't tell me who did it could you?' asked MacLeod.

'No, but I expect I'll know just after you,' Robert replied. He was not being sarcastic, merely speaking the truth.

MacLeod handed him a travel warrant, issued by the Strathclyde police for use on duty; it saved costs as the police negotiated a cheaper fare from the ferry company. If he had to pay the full fare he would have great difficulty in reclaiming the cost. MacLeod always kept a couple in the car just in case he needed them. Robert took it from him saying, 'There's another one of your lot near the front, I'll tell him you're here,' and began to whistle as he walked away.

MacLeod hated anyone being too lively in the mornings and Robert could get under his skin. He looked between the parked cars and saw the familiar face of Detective Sergeant John Milton walking somewhat unsteadily towards him. The sea was quite calm but the Western Ferry had just gone over the wake of their rivals, the Caledonian MacBrayne Black and White ferry, and it had caused the turbulence. John climbed into the passenger seat.

'Morning Boss, what's up? The young laddie has just told me about the body in the graveyard. I didn't expect to see you on this ferry.'

'What are you doing here?' MacLeod asked. He was pleased to see Detective Sergeant John Milton, his 'side-kick', 'bag-carrier' and good friend. John and Cameron had worked together for years and they were a good team.

'I went to a stag night last night and I missed the last ferry. I didn't fancy driving all the way round so I stayed at my daughters'. Now I'm off home,' said Milton. 'It's supposed to be my weekend off but I think you are going to need a little help!'

Although Gourock is only some twenty minutes by ferry from Dunoon, it is about a hundred-mile round trip over the Erskine Bridge, through Dumbarton, up Loch Lomond, through Arrochar and eventually passing Loch Eck into Dunoon. It is a beautiful drive passing through some of the most spectacular scenery in Scotland. At weekends the last ferry is at midnight and such a trek is not viewed with pleasure, therefore it is no surprise that the residents on the peninsular have friends or relatives who will happily give a bed when necessary.

'How do you manage to keep secrets around here?' asked MacLeod.

Milton looked at his boss with a startled look on his face, MacLeod had been brought up in the area. 'Perhaps you have been on the 'other side' of the water too long and you've forgotten your roots. You know there's no such thing as a secret, but there are some things that no-one talks about. Now, what should I know, Boss?'

MacLeod sighed. Perhaps he had been away too long, but Milton had to remember that he had left Dunoon as a young man, or more like a boy — he'd only been fifteen — to join the Army. It was a long time ago, another life away. Things had changed so much since then.

MacLeod told Milton the sketchy information he had and both men said little more. Long years of experience told both of them not to theorise about what they may find, any such speculation would be invariably wrong.

MacLeod left his car at the ferry car park and Sergeant Milton drove the few miles to Kilmun, past the Holy Loch where the American navy had been domiciled. The old houses have been reclaimed, painted and sold at a profit. One person's loss is always someone else's gain. The absence of the Americans is keenly felt by some, they brought young men with an abundance of energy and life, however the local boys were relieved when they did go. They had a charm which led to many of the prettiest girls in the locality becoming their wives.

On arrival at the locus they found that Sergeant Gillespie had efficiently and capably sorted out the mundane but vital aspects of any murder enquiry. Blue and white 'Police' tape sealed the entrance to a very small, pretty kirk that had a magnificent view over the Clyde estuary. A great deal of bustle and activity was evident by police and civilian workers alike.

MacLeod felt that the aftermath of a murder was just like throwing a smoke grenade into a beehive, the buzz was about the same. Two police cars were parked at the entrance to the church and there were small groups of smartly dressed people talking in hushed tones. Although they were talking quietly they looked shocked, and as they talked there was an air of excitement, nothing like this had happened around here before. They had come to church to pray but found more to do than the ritual cleansing of their souls.

Parked in the public car park near the entrance was a black hearse, two men were sitting in the front, an empty coffin in the back, patiently waiting for the experts to finish their work in order that they could take the cause of the unnatural activity away.

'Over here, Sir.' Sergeant Gillespie emerged from behind a group of parishioners and approached MacLeod. 'I'm so glad you're here, I have done everything I could but this is making me sick!'

MacLeod raised his eyebrows, 'Gillespie — sick?' he thought. 'Most unusual, he can usually take anything thrown at him!' He refrained from speaking his thoughts aloud.

'Show us the locus, please.'

'This way.' Gillespie led MacLeod and Milton through the gathering crowd at the gate.

'Get rid of these people,' hissed Milton to Gillespie; the latter had noted the irritation on MacLeod's face. He nodded.

'Who identified him?' asked MacLeod as he casually walked towards the grisly remains at the kirk.

'I did, not formally, but I know him well enough and even with the head missing I recognised him. I went back,' Gillespie shuddered, 'and I found his wallet with his driving licence, the key to the kirk was in his pocket.'

'Have you told the next of kin?' Milton asked.

'Yes, and I took WPC O'Neill with me. She'll look after Mrs Campbell; she was pretty hysterical and wanted to come to the church. Not a good idea!'

'Does Mrs Campbell know that the head is missing?' asked MacLeod.

'No. I hope we find it before we have to tell her.' MacLeod hoped so too.

As they neared the graveyard Sergeant Gillespie stopped. It was obvious to the two detectives that he felt unwell: apart from the fact that his face was grey, he swayed and appeared about to faint. He leant on the low wall to steady himself.

MacLeod put his hand on Gillespie's shoulder and said, 'You don't have to come any further, we'll go on ourselves.' He was genuinely concerned about Gillespie; MacLeod had never seen him so affected.

Gillespie gulped for air, then said, 'The police surgeon is with the body. Thanks for letting me stay; I'll be more use helping my

37

constables than here. Constable Murray is on the barrier and as he's a new boy, I think I'll supervise him and make sure he gets all the details of anyone coming through the barrier.'

It is necessary that everyone visiting the locus of the crime be logged and their details noted accurately and correctly with times and duration of their visit; purely as a precaution in the event of a gigantic cock-up and any compromising of the forensic evidence. It was handy to know where to start pointing the finger of blame. MacLeod grunted, which Gillespie took for consent, and left.

Milton walked behind MacLeod and tried to disturb as little of the scene as possible; but kept his eyes open. MacLeod saw a man in his late thirties with his back to him, leaning over the body of a fully clothed man lying on the grave. As he moved forward he recognised Doctor Ellis the local police surgeon.

'Can't you resuscitate him and we can all go home, Doc?' He had worked with Doctor Ellis before and there was a good rapport between them.

'Hardly Cameron, when there's no head.' Doctor Ellis looked up from his work and saw MacLeod's broad grin, then realised that MacLeod was trying to be amusing.

'Tut-tut! Such levity and on consecrated ground too.' Ellis stepped back and said, 'Have a look, it isn't a pretty sight.'

MacLeod bent over the body with his hands behind his back. He saw a long handled knife: it had two screws, one near the base and the other near the top of the handle. There was also a metal loop at the end of the handle.

'It isn't a kitchen knife anyway, I haven't seen a knife like that before.'

'Neither have I,' said Ellis. 'I will know more when I remove it at the lab. Are you coming to the PM?'

MacLeod ignored the question. Doctor Ellis was being sarcastic. He knew that MacLeod would duck that great pleasure and get one of his team to attend. He didn't mind looking at bodies, no matter what condition they were in, but he loathed seeing them cut up. They were always human beings to him, until that first cut when they became meat. He hated the shuddering transition he felt at the first violation of the body.

'When did it happen?' MacLeod asked.

'Well, I'm not sure, the slab is cold and that can affect my judgement but I suspect no more than ten hours ago, so that would be between nine and eleven last night, give or take an hour. We'll know more when we find the head, and after the post-mortem. I don't know what killed him; he was certainly dead before he was decapitated.'

'He was dead *before* his head was removed?' exclaimed Milton.

'Yes, there isn't enough blood around the gravestones for that to have been the cause of death, so go find the head,' replied Doctor Ellis.

'Was he killed here?' MacLeod was curious.

'Yes, I think so and he was decapitated here too. Look at the slab, there are some marks, recent cuts I shouldn't wonder, and it took two or three blows, maybe more, to get the head off.' Ellis was prodding the neck with a probe he had taken out from his bag. 'You know it isn't easy to decapitate anyone. If the neck is pulled back the muscles become taut and there's some force needed, alive or dead, to get a head off, or a really sharp knife. Even then it takes some strength.'

The knife in the stomach had taken MacLeod's attention. 'This knife?' he queried.

'Yes, it's possible,' Ellis sighed. 'They were certainly making sure, weren't they?'

'You think there is more than one perpetrator?' MacLeod asked.

'Oh yes, have a look at these.' Ellis pointed out some scrape marks on the ground. He

40

lifted one of the corpse's shoes. 'His shoes are very clean but there's some dirt and scrapes on them. He's been dragged. He was probably knocked unconscious first and then killed, but I can't tell you if his head was caved in or some other method used as yet, but it was here or hereabouts. It must have been more than one, he's a big man to drag and then lift, unless it was one very, very strong person.'

'I would think it was a man, I can't foresee any woman being strong enough,' said Milton.

'I don't know,' said Ellis. 'Have you looked at Helen MacDonald lately?'

MacLeod and Milton looked at each other and nearly laughed. Milton thought, 'Yes, she's strong enough, but who would have the nerve to ask her? Not me I'll leave that to the Boss.'

MacLeod looked back at the silent mutilated body of the Reverend William Campbell, and the smile on his lips froze. He was disturbed that a man of the cloth had been murdered and then his body defiled in such a manner.

'Doc, will you get fingerprints taken when you get him to the mortuary, and John, will you get something from his home for a comparison? I want to make sure it's him. No mistakes please.' MacLeod decided he had seen enough and he tapped Milton on the shoulder. 'Come on we've got work to do.'

They walked to the kirk and passed through the heavy oak doors, held open by their own weight.

MacLeod looked at the locks, 'It seems that these locks are used regularly. It could be that they have been left open since last night.' The cool air of the kirk flowed towards them; it was a pleasant coolness.

Milton took a deep breath and said, 'I'm back in my childhood, flowers and polish and a cold bum, that's the kirk. I must try to go more often.' MacLeod nodded in agreement. He wasn't particularly religious but, oddly, he found comfort in religious services.

'Look there,' said Milton. 'There's a pair of glasses under the pulpit.' He pointed to a pair of horn-rimmed glasses, lying on the floor; the left-hand lens was broken and stared emptily up at the two detectives.

'Don't touch, they could belong to the Reverend. Perhaps he was killed here and dragged out,' said MacLeod.

'Or staggered out on his own?' Milton suggested.

'Whatever. We must have the whole of the kirk checked.' MacLeod was always thorough.

As they walked away they were passed by three of the forensic team, clad in white overalls and wearing white gloves. MacLeod shuddered; he hated the way they dressed now. When he had been a young detective they had not been so fastidious and looked like people, normal clothes rubber gloves and the regulation black bag. To MacLeod the new breed of scientist appeared to have come out of a science fiction novel and was somehow vaguely inhuman. 'The price of progress, I suppose,' he thought. 'Everything is becoming remote and somewhat alien to normality'.

MacLeod said to the nearest member of the forensic team, a young man who appeared hardly out of school, 'Go over the kirk with a fine tooth comb.'

As he and Milton left, MacLeod missed the wry smile the young man gave to his colleagues. Policemen were always stating the obvious and this particular young man had heard it all before, he took no offence, they were only doing their job.

At the barrier tape MacLeod pulled Sergeant Gillespie to one side whilst Milton stood with Constable Murray to give the young officer a little support.

'I'm sorry, I understand why you didn't want to go back. It was very wise not to allow Mrs Campbell to see her husband. Sort out a search team once the forensics have finished. I want a fingertip search.' MacLeod was totally confident in Gillespie's abilities.

'Did the minister wear glasses?' asked MacLeod

'Yes, horn-rimmed ones I think. Why?' replied Gillespie.

'There's a broken pair in the kirk.'

'I hope not.' Gillespie was upset. 'I hope the kirk was not the place where he was killed. It would be desecration.'

'Now, tell me all you know of the Minster.' MacLeod wanted to get Gillespie's mind off the place where Campbell had died.

'Nothing much really when I come to think about it. He came here about sixteen years ago. He has four children. The eldest three, girls, are all married and live over the water. The youngest, Iain, is at University. I know he's home for the weekend; in fact he was in the cells for the night. I let him out with the other boy, Ewen Jones, this morning. Ewen reported the death; his mother found the body. After I called you out she went into shock and I called her doctor. This is a bad business.'

'What on earth did they do to spend an uncomfortable night in your cells?' MacLeod asked. 'Not a lot really, they were drunk and making a noise in Argyll Street in Dunoon. They were throwing mud at the CCTV and you know the latest instruction on unruly behaviour. Well, they had to be locked up. This morning after they had apologised I read them their fortune, cautioned them and sent them on their way. Neither had been in trouble before so I thought it best.'

MacLeod could only agree. He thought of his own youth and was pleased that surveillance cameras had not been invented then. He would surely have been in the same position as these boys if they had been installed. He did not know that Gillespie was thinking exactly the same thing. Eric Gillespie remembered the time he had shinned up a lamppost to remove a bulb just because he 'felt like it'. Youthful transgressions can bring a flush to the face, even in middle age.

'Thank you Sergeant. I'll have to see the Fiscal and tell him about this. It would be nice to be first for a change. I won't be long; the rest of the team should have turned up by the time I get back. By the way, where have you set up the incident room?'

Gillespie said, 'In the hall round the back of the kirk. I have contacted the curator. It won't be used for anything now, so it is available. I've got hold of British Telecom to put in the extra lines we will need. We could be ready by midday.'

'Fine,' said MacLeod. 'I'll leave everything to you. Come on John,' he said over his shoulder to Detective Sergeant Milton. 'Take me to the Fiscal's house.' As he turned to go he said to Gillespie, 'By the way, who opened the kirk doors?'

'I don't know, they were open when I got here and Mrs Jones didn't get that far,' said Gillespie.

'Hello Mr MacLeod.' A strident female voice was heard above the babble of voices. MacLeod looked round and saw Helen MacDonald. 'Oh dear me!' he said when he recognised her. He turned to Gillespie and said, 'I'm off, head her off for me,' and almost ran to Milton's car, closely followed by the woman whom he feared more than anyone, though he would never admit to it.

Helen was very strong and tenacious when she needed to be, and in her job it was a distinct advantage. She had cornered MacLeod more than once, much to his regret. She would have made a fine detective had she chosen that career and then MacLeod would have shown respect, but even then he would have been nervous of her.

Sergeant Gillespie stepped in front of Helen as she bore down on her quarry, allowing his escape. Detective Sergeant Milton had seen

46

Helen MacDonald a split second before his boss and had got to the car and started the engine, ready to get away as fast as possible. He was as wary of Helen as MacLeod, and knew a quick escape was in order.

As MacLeod climbed into the passenger seat Milton risked a facetious comment. 'What kept you?'

4

Mrs Julia Campbell was sitting in the living room of the large draughty Manse; she was surrounded by half packed boxes. Her son Iain was in the kitchen making a cup of tea, the cups clattered in the distance. WPC Margaret O'Neill sat on a lounge seat leaning forward, her face showed concern but she refrained from offering a comforting hand. Mrs Campbell's demeanour prevented any physical contact.

Julia couldn't believe that her husband was dead. She had wished it many times throughout their marriage in the heat of anger at his latest escapade, but she loved him and had forgiven him so many times. She was going over in her mind the first time they had met and the first years of their marriage. It was difficult to keep the tears at bay but she succeeded.

Now everything would have to come out, her children would know about their father and, worst of all, the neighbours would know and give her those sympathetic looks and smiles which she simply couldn't bear. How unfeeling of him, even in death he had to be flamboyant. She just sat, she couldn't speak. It wasn't as if she was unwilling to speak, she literally could not speak. It was her reaction to grief. Her left side felt so cold. She wasn't paralysed, she knew that, it was as if someone had cut her body in half and taken it away.

Iain came into the room carrying a tray with three cups of tea, too full. He had managed to slop tea into all three saucers. His mother gave him an exasperated look, which made him even more nervous.

Julia tried to say 'thank you' as he handed her a cup, but nothing came out of her mouth. She shook her head and finally allowed the tears to flow. She missed her husband and wanted to howl her grief to the world, but she merely sat on the couch and stared into the middle distance. She saw him as he was on their wedding day, dressed in his Campbell tartan, so strong and so . . . the only word she could find was beautiful. He was beyond handsome in her eyes with his shock of dark hair tinged with red.

Julia had forgotten what she had thought when he left the house. Remembering the early part of their marriage when she really had loved him, and, she believed, he really had loved her, gave her comfort.

Iain knelt down on the floor at his mother's

knee. He put his head in her lap and she absent-mindedly put her hand on his dark head of hair, so like his father's, and twisted the locks in her fingers. Mothering instinct took over and she began to rock her body backwards and forwards humming to calm her child. It was the first sound she had made since being awoken and told about her husband's death.

WPC O'Neill found the scene disturbing, but could not think of anything to say to stop the eerie sound coming from Mrs Campbell's lips. Although she had comforted many families in grief, she could not penetrate the wall between herself and her charges; she had never seen such depth of emotion. She hoped that sometime later she could find the words she needed to do her job properly.

Detective Sergeant Milton dropped MacLeod off at the home of the Procurator Fiscal and went back to the church to organise the incident room. Scottish law differs dramatically from English Law inasmuch as it is the Procurator Fiscal who is charged with the prosecution of offenders and he or she alone determines whether a crime has been committed. The Fiscal then directs the police, as their agents, to investigate any alleged crimes. All crimes have to be reported to the Fiscal as soon as possible and the Fiscal can and often does direct the way an investigation proceeds.

In English law the police have the duty to investigate crime and the Crown Prosecution Service then decide whether there is enough evidence to prosecute. Rarely does the Crown Prosecution Service get involved with an investigation.

Detective Chief Inspector Cameron MacLeod and his friend Duncan Grey, the Procurator Fiscal for the area, sat in the lounge of a fine Victorian House situated on the sea front at Strone some two miles from where the Reverend William Campbell was lying in an unceremonial state. Duncan was wearing a thick brocade dressing gown, having been aroused from a deep sleep by the incessant knocking at the door. He had been a little grumpy when he answered the door, but he knew immediately on seeing MacLeod's grey face that there was something seriously wrong.

MacLeod was quickly ushered into the reception room. In the past this would have been referred to as the 'drawing room', but not now, with its trappings of television set, CD player and obvious continual family use. 'Drawing room' was a phrase from another era.

'I can't believe it Cameron, Bill was a good

man. We don't go to the kirk as much as we should, but we knew him well and I always found him a good man.' He paused, trying to collect his thoughts. 'Dead you say, and murdered too! How did it happen?'

MacLeod told Grey as much as he knew and saw the other man's eyes widen in shock. 'When did it happen?'

'Late last night. Doctor Ellis thinks sometime between nine and eleven, but gave the usual proviso, give or take a few hours, and if you are going to ask if we have any suspects, don't. John and I have just got here and the rest of the team haven't arrived and I know nothing about the man or his background.'

'It wasn't that, I thought I may be able to help. Much as I don't want to get involved I think I must. There have been rumours about him. You see, he was supposed to be a ladies man, very discreet you know, but in a small community like this everyone knows everyone else's business. I heard that he had had a fling with a local lady. Not that I know who she was, you understand,' said Grey.

'If you don't know, can you give me a hint who would? It would be a great help.' MacLeod appreciated Grey telling him immediately where to start, he had found in the past that so often friends will not come forward with essential information in a misguided attempt to protect their families.

'My secretary of course. What Maureen Stewart doesn't know about the local community isn't worth knowing.' Grey smiled. Maureen was the salt of the earth and knew almost everything about everyone on the peninsula, and she collected gossip like others collected stamps.

'Thank you for that. Could you give me her home telephone number and I'll get someone onto it right away. I think it would be better to send a woman, give her an excuse to have a good gossip.' MacLeod sensed that anything Maureen Stewart could say would be of great assistance. Once he had a motive for the murder he could then set out to find the killer or killers.

'Cameron, you male chauvinist pig, I hope none of your lot hear you talking like that,' said Grey. 'Not at all, it's horses for courses, I know when to use my staff to the best advantage. If I had a man on the team who could get information through a good gossip like my women then I would use him, but I haven't, so I don't. Keep my reasons between ourselves. In this politically correct society I'm known as a dinosaur. I think that's what I overheard. It's a more polite term than some of the things that have been said

53

about me.' MacLeod laughed out loud.

'Cameron, find his head. I feel quite unwell about this. I promise you I won't go to the locus, I'm horrified by it all.' The Fiscal had every right to visit the locus of a crime but rarely exercised that right, normally they had enough to do without cluttering up their day with unnecessary trips out of the office. They had faith in the police to do their job right.

MacLeod, on returning to the locus, went straight to the church hall, whose name was now known to all and sundry as the incident room. It had been completely taken over, the only sign of ecumenical occupation being the children's drawings on one wall depicting Christ in bold colourful crayon. MacLeod was pleased to see that the BT men were in the last throes of installing the telephone lines. The hall was not a large one but adequate for the purpose. There was a small room off the main hall, which had been set up as his office. It was well known that he needed a separate office in which to think and be peaceful. There was a distinct smell of fresh coffee.

Detective Sergeant John Milton emerged from behind a screen with a steaming mug in his hand. 'Here you are, Boss. I thought you may need this.' He thrust a tartan ceramic mug of coffee into MacLeod's hand.

MacLeod took the mug and warmed his hands on the porcelain. He looked at the 'posh' mug and noted it was Dunoon Pottery with a Stewart tartan imprinted on the outside. 'My, we are coming up in the world, what happened to the chipped mug I usually get?'

'These are complements of Charlie Steele, the curator. He took one look at our box of mugs and said we would get a disease from them and produced half a dozen of these. If we break any we have to replace them. I can always nip down to the factory and get another if that happens.'

MacLeod sipped the hot liquid gratefully. Somehow tea and coffee tasted better from porcelain. Although it was summer the hall felt chilly. He looked around; gradually his team were arriving.

Detective Inspector Peter Reade, immaculate as always, looked as though he had just stepped out of a tailor's window. Detective Inspector Janet MacBain was the opposite, with little dress sense, her suit smart but too old for her. MacLeod wished she would dress more suitably for her age, she was thirty going on fifty by her clothing. Even her handbag and shoes did not match and the scarf she wore was too bright for the rest of her outfit.

MacLeod sighed; she was the best detective on his team but certainly didn't look it.

Detective Constable Frank Morris was busily attending to his beloved computers, his owlish appearance enhanced by a suntan recently acquired in Barbados. He had quietly slipped away and married his long-term girlfriend, much to the chagrin of his family and colleagues alike. It wasn't the fact that he had slipped away, it was that he had done them out of a celebration, an excuse to have a party. No matter, he would be suitably 'sent off' to his marriage by a surprise party, when he least expected it. It would embarrass him horribly but traditions are not easily broken, no matter how shy and retiring a person may be.

MacLeod wondered if Janet would do the same when her time came, thinking she should hurry up or she would be 'left on the shelf'. Imprinting of youth is difficult to shake off; he could not get it out of his head that a woman could only be fulfilled within the confines of marriage. Fortunately he had never expressed such a sentiment to her, or he would have felt the lash of her tongue, Janet was perfectly content as she was, her own flat, car and company when she wanted it. She didn't have any ambition to be a mother despite her homely figure; she wasn't comfortable with children.

No such thoughts came into MacLeod's head when Detective Sergeant Susan Lampart arrived. He knew she was a lesbian and was living with an older policewoman, no matter how hard she tried to keep the fact secret. MacLeod had no prejudice about anyone's sexuality provided they were a good officer, but he did wonder about homosexuals. His heterosexuality was certain but he could not imagine a man in love with another man — women he understood, but not men. Susan was a very attractive woman and had been married, producing two children. He often wondered what had been done to cause her to change sides, so to speak. He would never pry into the whys and wherefores, it was not his way.

He turned to Detective Sergeant Milton and said, 'Get the team together, we'll have a briefing of what we know.'

'MacPherson hasn't arrived yet, perhaps we should give him a few more minutes?'

Morris overheard. 'He won't be here for a while Sir, he rang and said he is having problems with a baby-sitter, it's his weekend with the kids.'

MacPherson had recently separated from his wife and he had access to his children on alternate weekends. MacLeod considered this for a moment. 'Ring him, tell him I'll see him tomorrow, he will have to catch up quickly.'

MacLeod was very happily married but had seen many marriages and careers affected by the pressure of police work. Although he should have insisted on MacPherson being here, he remembered a time years ago in his career when one of his daughters had been very ill and he had asked for a few days off to be with her. He had been told that he had a job to do and his family should come second. It was the nearest he'd ever got to resigning. He vowed that if he ever became a senior officer he would never lose a good officer because of petty rules. He could do without MacPherson for a while.

The team of such dissimilar people had gelled together well and MacLeod had insisted that if he were ever in charge of any serious case he would have this team, and only this team as his own. He remembered with a smile his reluctance to take the two women at first; it was only because he hadn't chosen them. He had had to mentally eat his own words after they had been with his core detectives for a mere day. He approved of them, both as team members and people.

MacLeod briefed the team as quickly as he could. As he was briefing his officers a flustered police motorcyclist arrived with a large brown envelope containing rush photographs of the murdered man and the interior of the kirk.

'This will make life easier,' he said as he pinned them onto the wall. He turned round to see Detective Inspector Reade turn his head away. Both Detective Inspector MacBain and Detective Sergeant Lampart were standing stock still, a look of horror on their faces. To his surprise Detective Constable Morris showed no emotion at all. 'I thought *he* would be the one to throw up,' thought MacLeod. 'Perhaps I have severely misjudged him.' What MacLeod did not notice was that young Morris had glanced at the first picture and swiftly removed his glasses: he could not now see the pictures and therefore gave the appearance of nonchalance.

'It looks like someone didn't want him identified quickly, but that's impossible. He was a big man and his wallet and driving licence were left in his pocket,' said Morris, talking as if to himself.

'Why would he be dragged from the kirk and mutilated there?' Susan had turned back after gaining control of herself and was looking at the photograph of the interior of the kirk. She pointed to the candlesticks on the altar and said 'That candlestick is out of line.'

MacLeod looked over her shoulder. 'So it is, no doubt the forensic boys have taken it away for tests.'

'I suppose it is him?' asked Janet MacBain. 'We are getting fingerprints from his house, and whoever goes to the PM will have to get fingerprints from the cadaver. We'll be sure then,' replied Macleod.

'But why take the head, some bizarre ritual or what?' asked Detective Sergeant Susan Lampart.

'More to the point, where is the dammed head?' said MacLeod. 'It isn't logical, but then, when is murder ever logical? This is a weird one.'

'Do we know anything about this man?' asked Janet MacBain.

'I think his lifestyle could be suspect,' said MacLeod. 'And I think you could be the ideal person to find out. Here's a contact, the Fiscal's secretary, Mrs Maureen Stewart.' He handed Janet a piece of paper with a telephone number on it. 'Give her a ring and make an appointment.'

MacLeod turned to Morris. 'Find out about his life from that thing.' He pointed to the computer. 'I don't just want the bare facts, I want interviews set up with friends and relatives so we can get some idea of what he was about.'

MacLeod disliked computers and mistrusted them. In his view too many cases had been actively delayed by the reliance on the facts spewed out by them. Sometimes mistakes were made. He checked and re-checked everything. He acknowledged that computers could be invaluable at times but he didn't know of any computer that went out and felt a collar.

'Detective Sergeant Lampart, sort out house to house enquires.'

'What staff do we have available?' Lampart replied.

'I don't know yet,' said Detective Inspector Peter Reade, 'I saw Sergeant Gillespie when I came in and he said he would give us his men once the search of the area has been done.'

'I don't think we will have to drag anything out of anyone, this has shocked everyone and the neighbours will be queuing up to talk. I'll get a checklist together,' said Detective Sergeant Lampart.

'Do we know the time scale?' asked Detective Constable Morris.

'The doctor said roughly sometime between nine and eleven last night. Once we find out what time he left home I think anytime from then. Mrs Campbell is in total shock at the moment, perhaps a discreet visit may help,' replied Detective Sergeant Milton.

Detective Inspector Reade asked with resignation in his voice, 'Am I the office manager again?'

'Too right,' said MacLeod, 'you are the best one I have. I know I promised that you could do some outside work, but I really need you in the office. You can see that.'

Detective Inspector Reade was pleased with the compliment but was still a little upset. He knew he was a good administrator but he wanted to be a great detective. He would get his time, he was sure of that, but *when?* He suddenly came out of his reverie to hear a pleasing exchange: he was relieved to know he wouldn't have to attend the post-mortem.

'You will be glad to know that Detective Inspector MacBain and Detective Sergeant Lampart have drawn the short straws this time. They will attend the post-mortem, which is due,' MacLeod looked at his watch, 'in about half an hour so get your skates on.'

'No, Sir! I hate post-mortems.' Janet nearly spilt her coffee as she jerked upright in her chair.

'None of us like them,' he growled. The

two detectives looked at each other and decided that any arguments were futile; MacLeod's tone of voice ensured that they would do as he said.

'Well?' MacLeod said to Susan Lampart.

'I never uttered a stutter, Boss,' she said and turned to Janet MacBain, 'I think we should be going, don't you?'

Janet grimaced and said, 'I suppose we had better get it over with.' They picked up their handbags and left the room.

MacLeod looked at his notes. The room was very quiet, awaiting any further instructions. MacLeod was in a strange mood; he was demanding at times but mostly allowed his staff freedom to work on their own. He felt that too many restrictions on his staff stifled creativity and imagination, absolutely essential qualities for good detectives. MacLeod was disturbed at this murder; he was not a churchgoing Christian but he believed in God and his youthful upbringing instilled a set of values in him by which he tried to live. It was the murder of a Minister that had set his teeth on edge, a man of God, and he didn't want his team to find out the depth of his abhorrence of this crime. Once he got used to the idea he would revert to his normal self, but for now he had to keep the team at arm's length and the only way he knew how to do that was to become a bit of a grizzly bear.

'Right, we are going to see the woman who found the body. Come on.' MacLeod touched Detective Sergeant Milton's shoulder; John put his coffee cup down and followed him. As they left MacLeod said to no-one in particular. 'Get on with it. You 'armchair' detectives will have to show something when we get back.'

5

Detective Inspector Janet MacBain and Detective Sergeant Susan Lampart were standing in the pristine clean mortuary, shrouded in white coats, white mask and wearing white wellingtons. They were to witness the autopsy of William Campbell, what there was left of him that is.

The sickly smell permeating the room was a mixture of cheap air spray and formaldehyde; the combination was unpleasant but bearable. The lighting was harsh on the white walls and stainless steel furniture, enhanced by ultra-violet light to kill whatever dangerous germs were left after the thorough cleaning of the mortuary, which took place at regular intervals. The cadaver was naked, lying on its back on a stainless steel bench.

The clothes had been removed by the mortuary attendant, Harry, a man of slight build and in middle age, who seemed unsuited for this kind of work. Moving bodies requires a great deal of strength: once air has been expelled from the body and it becomes inert, the subsequent effect is dramatic on the weight of a cadaver, it becomes very heavy.

Harry was a great deal stronger than he looked, and he wore an expression of deep reverence, which suited his job exactly, but it covered a warped sense of humour, which was not in keeping with the sombre work he performed. He took great care over the deceased, treating him or her with respect and some tenderness, always bearing in mind the sensitivities of the relatives.

Harry had no such respect for laboratory technicians or new police officers who fell into his clutches and had, at least on one occasion, arranged for the lights to go out, leaving the eerie blue ultra-violet lights remaining. He once lay on the bench covered with a shroud. After the lights were extinguished he slowly sat up, emitting a deep-throated moan. The unfortunate technician, of only some months standing, ran screaming from the room and was never seen again.

Fortunately no-one 'bubbled' Harry and the chief technician put the flight of the technician as a case of unsuitability for the type of work and nothing more was said. Harry did learn from this, he quite liked the young man and ensured that his jokes were perpetrated on less sensitive souls. Hovering over the body was the police photographer. In total contrast to Harry, Mark had recently qualified and this was the first time he had worked on his own. When he was told about the job he had to do he briefly thought about asking someone else to cover for him but knew it was his bad luck and he had to get on with it. He regretted being on call this particular weekend.

Mark felt nauseous. The white coat he wore was too big for him and he had pulled the mask up his face, almost covering it, in a vain attempt to mask the smells. He would take as many photographs as he could to make sure that he missed nothing.

'Ready,' said Doctor Ellis as he walked into the room. He was pulling on his rubber gloves, which he snapped around his wrists. 'Shall we begin?' Tugging at the knife he said, 'Lets get this out.' But the knife was stuck fast.

'That makes life more difficult, it will have to be done the hard way,' he said as he took up a scalpel to cut the flesh of the torso.

Harry looked at the two detectives and saw interest in their faces. He sighed, knowing that neither woman was at all squeamish and nothing he could do would phase them. No, these two would take anything he could give and probably give back more. He mentally crossed them off his list of victims.

At the conclusion of the autopsy a strangely

shaped knife, some nine inches in length, was lying on the bench near the sink. Doctor Ellis hosed it down using a rubber tube connected to a U-shaped tap over the stainless steel sink. Water splashed everywhere.

'I thought at first that maybe this knife couldn't have been used to decapitate the victim, but let me see.' He gripped the knife firmly by the handle and brandished it in the air. 'See, it's like a machete.' He put the blade near the cut marks on the neck. 'Yes, this is it, look at the cuts — fits beautifully.'

'Beautifully' was not the word either of the detectives would have used in the circumstances.

Suddenly, Doctor Ellis put the knife down and jerked the overhead light sharply down towards the body and illuminated the severed neck. He peered intently at the cuts. Both women leant over his shoulder, Janet on his left and Susan on his right.

'Yes, yes, that's it,' he said.

'What? What do you see?' asked Janet.

'Here.' He pointed to faint bruising near one of the cuts. 'He was strangled first, there's a clear mark, finger marks I think, but I'm afraid there won't be any prints, there's too much damage by the knife.'

Ellis turned to the photographer. 'Get some

photos of the bruising, it may help.' The youth gulped and leant over, concentrating on the mechanics of photography rather than what he was photographing.

Harry saw Mark's reaction and smiled to himself. 'Now here is a new victim,' he thought. 'Must arrange something for him the next time he visits.'

'So, he was strangled and then his head cut off. Why did the murderer stab him afterwards?' Susan was bemused.

'I have no idea, but once the knife was in the body the killer would never have been able to get it out, it was jammed between two vertebrae. It must have been done with considerable force, I had enough problems getting it out,' said Doctor Ellis.

'What about the time of death?' asked Janet.

'Oh, about ten last night, give or take an hour, maybe earlier. The stone slab would have cooled the body quicker.' He paused for a few seconds and then went on. 'It's funny, he was dead at least fifteen minutes before he was decapitated. Look at the severed neck.' He pointed to the jagged bloody flesh. 'Blood is congealed, it didn't spurt and splash everywhere when the head was cut off. It would have saturated the ground a considerable distance from the body. From the gore I saw on the ground in globules, the blood had to have congealed before he was decapitated. It takes at least fifteen minutes for that to happen. He could have been dead up to and no later than an hour before his head was cut off. After that the blood will separate and liquefy again. There's too little loss in the body too.'

Janet, for the first time, felt queasy.

'Get the head for me and I will be able to tell you the cause of death,' said Doctor Ellis. He was completely unconcerned by the reaction of his audience.

Janet nodded, hoping someone else would find the head. It was spooky: a man was murdered then mutilated some time later. What on earth was the murderer doing in those fifteen minutes to an hour? Going for the knife perhaps?

'Could you take his fingerprints for us?' Susan was hopeful.

'No lass, that's your job, so get on with it quickly so we can all go home.'

'Not us I'm afraid,' said Janet.

Harry handed Susan the box containing the fingerprint equipment kept at the mortuary by the coroner's officer, and he helped her take the cadaver's fingerprints. Difficult as it is to take good prints from co-operative human beings, she almost had to break his

70

fingers to separate them. The effect of rigor mortis had not worn off.

When they were getting into the car some ten minutes later, Janet turned to Susan, as she put the evidence bags containing Reverend Campbell's clothes and the knife on the back seat, and said, 'Whoever did this wasn't taking any chances. I hope I don't meet them on a dark night.'

★ ★ ★

Mrs Grace Jones was sitting in the kitchen of her small but neat home. She had her head cupped in her hands, the mug of coffee in front of her slowly going cold. Her doctor, Doctor Moorbath, had just left. She was staring at the two small tablets he had left on the table. She wondered what had come over him. Doctor Moorbath was of the old school, he didn't believe in tranquillisers and had told her she should go through this without drugs. She had not asked him for anything, but he had produced these pills to allow her to get one good night's sleep. He told her to throw them away if she didn't need them, but that was all he was prepared to give her.

Doctor Moorbath believed that there was a natural process the body had to go through

71

and giving pills only delayed matters. He had no tranquilliser junkies on his books. He was the darling of the health service, he never prescribed drugs unless absolutely necessary, and he had not done so now. Grace would never know that he had left a placebo, she had already decided to flush them down the loo.

Ewen, her son, was looking at her from the doorway of the kitchen.

'Mum, please lie down, you don't look very well. If you need anything I will get it for you.' Ewen loved his mother very much, despite her nagging. 'Do you get enough to eat?' was her first cry when he came home from University. If she only knew how many girls fed him. He was pampered and well cared for. It was his air of vulnerability that attracted them and he carefully cultivated his helplessness. He didn't want the girls to know that his Mum had taught him to cook, sew, wash and iron, none of which he liked doing but did as well as anyone when he had to.

Grace wearily straightened up and said, 'I'm all right now, stop fussing. You sound like your grandmother.'

Ewen suddenly had an idea. 'OK, but if you don't lie down, I'll ring Gran and tell her what is happening and she'll be over as soon as I put the phone down.'

'Blackmailer, you wouldn't.' Grace relaxed and grimaced. She didn't want her mother here. A formidable lady of 72, she brooked no nonsense from anyone. Grace was as nervous of her in one of her crusading moods as any stroppy minor official or shopkeeper would be, meeting her mother in full flight.

'I would,' said Ewen. 'Now come on.'

He escorted her to the lounge where she sat on the couch with her feet up. He removed her fluffy pink slippers, carefully placing them side by side on the floor. As he put them down he smiled. His Mum was strong and sensible but she had her 'fluffy' moments and these slippers were just perfect for that part of her. He put a tartan rug over her and went to close the curtains. As he looked out of the window he saw two men walking up the path. Both were tall and well built. One was wearing a blue pinstripe suit, the other grey flannels and a blue blazer. He reckoned that they were in their late forties or early fifties. 'Police' was written all over them. They didn't need a uniform to give that certain air of officialdom.

'Mum, I think the police are here, should I send them away?' asked Ewen.

'No, I'm all right, let them in.' Grace

was relieved she had something to do. This concern for her welfare by her son was becoming overwhelming, she was beginning to feel like an invalid and that was the last thing she wanted.

Detective Inspector MacLeod and Detective Sergeant Milton were seated in the parlour with cups of tea in their hands. Both felt uncomfortable in the flowered bamboo lounge chairs. It had crossed both of their minds that these seats were not designed for men of their stature and they fervently hoped there would be no disasters. MacLeod noted that Grace was clearly shaken but trying not to show it. He was also well aware that her son, Ewen, was hovering nearby, his hostility clearly showing.

'What can I do for you?' asked Mrs Jones.

'Do you feel up to talking about it this morning,' enquired MacLeod.

'Carry on, I will have to talk about it sometime,' said Grace.

'Could you describe how you found the minister?' asked MacLeod.

'Are you sure it is him?' Grace prayed it was not him. She had a great deal of affection for the man and the manner of his departure from this world was not something she wanted to dwell on.

'Oh yes, I'm afraid there's no doubt,' said Milton as gently as possible.

'I've already told the others, I went to church early to arrange the flowers and as I got to the doors I saw him.' She shuddered. Picking up a packet of cigarettes she lit one and inhaled deeply, looking around for an ashtray.

'Here you are.' Ewen sounded petulant as he handed her an ashtray, a souvenir from France. 'I wish you wouldn't smoke.'

'Don't go on, I may have given up years ago but I can't stand being nagged. If no-one smoked, who would pay the extra taxes? When you start work and actually start paying taxes you will know what I mean. It's my life and I'll do what I like with it. Anyway the way things are smoking and shortening my life is a positive benefit to the country. I won't be a burden on the State for too long. If I gave up smoking it would cost the Government a fortune in pension if I lived longer.' Grace gave him a 'mother's look' that brooked no argument.

Ewen shook his head and turned away. He hated it when she even referred to her death. He loved her dearly and he really wanted her to get a telegram from the Queen.

MacLeod smiled. He enjoyed a cigar but had the same type of conversation with his eldest daughter Jacqueline when he smoked one in her presence, which wasn't often. He too believed that everyone had the right to live their own lives their own way provided no-one else was hurt. He thought that drinkers should be attacked more than smokers, after all, when was the last time he heard the defence in court that the accused had committed the crime because he had smoked twenty cigarettes too many, instead of having too much to drink? Life would be so boring if everyone was the same.

'Did you know Mr Campbell well?' said MacLeod, trying to break the wall of silence that had unexpectedly been erected in the room.

'He was my minister and I did some things for the kirk, he was a very nice man. He always made time for me, especially when my marriage broke down some years ago.' She turned to Ewen and said, 'Will you go down to the shop and get some milk? It will be open now. I forgot to get any yesterday.'

'But there's nearly a pint in the fridge, Mum.'

'Yes I know, but your sister is coming with the family and I expect we will get some other visitors apart from these gentlemen.'

'In that case I'll get two pints.'

Ewen left and Grace turned to the two officers and said, 'Quickly, while he's out. William comforted me. It sort of developed. We tried to keep it a secret but I know there are some suspicious nosy parkers in the village who suspected and will take great pleasure in telling you.'

MacLeod and Milton were taken aback by Grace's candour. There was a momentary silence whilst they took in the information. 'When did you start this affair?' asked Milton.

'It wasn't a full-blown affair, he sent me flowers and poems,' she sighed. 'He was so romantic. It was about four years ago, just after my daughter married and Ewen was taking his exams, when my ex-husband took off with his secretary. No warning, nothing. We had a big house in Strachur, so I sold up. William was a good friend and helped me find this house.' She paused and said, 'It wasn't a sexual affair, we didn't go to bed together, it would have spoiled everything if we had.' She looked at MacLeod with a steady gaze, almost defiantly.

'You have never been to bed with him?' MacLeod was incredulous.

'We nearly did, but I thought it would complicate things and as I didn't want anything permanent I thought it best not to. I enjoyed his company and was flattered by his attention, but I thought he would cause me problems if we went to bed. Sex isn't everything you know. I have built a new life, I like having control over my life, doing what I want to do. It may not be exciting but it's what I want. Is that so strange?'

Grace looked directly at MacLeod. He was still trying to come to terms with a relationship that was loving yet had not been consummated. He tried to imagine it but could not visualise it. He was too much of a male where he expressed his love physically; the romantic stuff embarrassed him.

'Oh, no, I suppose not,' he stuttered.

'Anyway, we stopped seeing so much of each other a few years ago.' Grace went on. 'It was for the best really.'

'Why was that?' MacLeod was now very curious.

'It was mainly me. We had to stop or go further. Stopping was easier. I began to think about his wife. He told me they hadn't slept together for years. I didn't like her but she was still his wife. It had happened to me and I wouldn't have been able to look her in the face if we had made love. I'm not dishonest and you cannot keep a secret like that.'

'Did you see him last night?' MacLeod brought the subject back to the case in hand.

He had to pry into other people's lives to make sense of a crime, in fact he had to enquire about sex lives. The most powerful motive of all was jealousy. He didn't have to like that part of his investigation, just get on with it. He knew of others who positively revelled in this aspect of detective work. They got a salacious kick out of it all, but not MacLeod, he was a normal man, pornography did not interest him.

'No, I thought I might out of the window, but I didn't see anyone. It was raining too hard.'

MacLeod listened intently to the way Grace spoke and believed she was not telling lies. She was incapable of lying but she was being economical with the truth.

MacLeod asked, 'Did you feel he had met someone else?'

Grace thought for a second. 'Well, maybe he had but I've no idea who it was. Come to think of it, yes, I think he probably had met someone. He was in love with love, if you know what I mean. Sex really didn't come into it, I think it was the chase he adored, rather than the capture.'

Milton was taking notes and raised his head. 'Why didn't you like Mrs Campbell?' he asked quietly.

'No particular reason, I always felt she

looked down her nose at me. I wasn't good enough for her.' Grace was about to say more when the door clicked and the sound of rushing young feet echoed throughout the house. She said urgently, 'Ewen is back, change the subject. If I think of anything else I'll come to you. Please keep everything I've told you to yourselves, I have my family to think about you know.'

They walked to the door and Mrs Grace Jones showed them out. She leant on the door jam. The whole of the morning had left her emotionally and physically drained. She decided to take her son's advice and lie down for a while, maybe she would feel better soon.

As they left to return to the incident room, MacLeod turned to Milton and said, 'Do you think she knew who the new love was?'

Milton thought for a second and replied, 'No I don't think so, he seems to have been a secretive man. Perhaps he got a kick out of having close secrets, and chasing women too.'

MacLeod wondered aloud. 'I wonder if they really didn't have sex.'

Milton thought about Mrs Jones, an attractive woman, handsome he thought. He couldn't imagine a deep relationship without expressing that love by making love.

'I don't know,' MacLeod said. 'Perhaps they didn't but there is only one person who can really tell us and he's dead.

'Do you think she could have killed him?' asked Milton.

'Possibly but she would need help. Get a check done, find out what time her son was arrested last night, his alibi may be too convenient.' MacLeod thought it unlikely but everything needed checking.

6

The incident room was very quiet except for the computer purring in the corner whilst Detective Constable Morris stared intently at the screen, his hands expertly zinging across the keyboard. Detective Inspector Reade was occupied with administration, piles of paperwork in front of him at his desk. He had three trays in front of him, IN, OUT and FIND OUT. He was a fussy man and would not answer any questions unless he truly had the right answer. Never one to waffle an answer the third tray was useful to him.

The door burst open and Mrs Helen MacDonald, the local reporter from the Dunoon and Argyllshire Standard appeared, her bulk almost filling the doorway. A young fresh-faced constable, Morris's face flushed with frustration and embarrassment plucked at her elbow and was being ignored completely. 'You can't go in there, we are taking all statements out here.' His voice was pleading; he glanced at Detective Inspector Reade, his eyes begging for help.

'It's all right, let her in,' said Reade.

Previous experience with our Helen, the Wicked Witch of the West, taught him that she had to be dealt with firmly and this young man was no match for her. His own last encounter had not been pleasant; she had neatly sidestepped him and information had appeared in the newspaper, which he had sorely tried not to give out, thus causing an uproar in the office. He sighed inwardly, but was determined to keep the upper hand this time. Once she had her foot in the door there was no stopping her, except by violence. Reade dismissed the idea of forcible removable; he eyed her size and thought he would not be strong enough even with Morris's help.

Helen flopped on the chair in front of Reade and busily rifled through her large raffia shopping bag for her notebook, Reade quietly sat, tapping his pen on the blotting paper in front of him waiting for the inevitable questions. He glanced over to Morris and saw that Morris's neck was turning a pink colour, the flush deepening. The latter frantically concentrated on his machine. All strong women made him nervous and he appeared like a frightened rabbit. Helen was one of the worst kind, she brought out his stutter as well.

Helen made herself comfortable. Turning

to Reade she said, 'I've already given a statement to the boys outside, but they didn't seem to want to know anything else, so I thought I would come and tell you myself.'

'Now I know you Mrs MacDonald.' Detective Inspector Reade was always formal in his dealings with the public. 'You want a story and you think I will give you one, but whatever you and I talk about here is confidential. You are a witness and you cannot publish anything about this case without the Fiscal's approval. You understand?' He emphasised the word 'understand'.

Helen looked distinctly uncomfortable. 'I suppose I can say he was murdered.'

'Yes, but that's all. No details please, you nearly ruined one investigation by being too outspoken. You aren't going to interfere this time, I promise you. If it hadn't been for Mr MacLeod the Fiscal would have prosecuted you.' Reade spoke with firmness bordering on rudeness but he thought it was the only way to get through to this strident female.

Helen was stunned. MacLeod had intervened on her behalf. She thought he hated her, after all he was always avoiding her. She mentally shrugged and said, 'I understand, but I have some local

84

information I think you need. I know it sounds silly but when I was told about his head, well it's strange, but did you know that Sir Duncan Campbell of Lochaw founded this kirk in 1442? In 1661 the then Marquis of Argyll was executed for treason and his head was displayed in Edinburgh, on the ramparts. It wasn't until 1664 that his head was re-united with his body and buried in the mausoleum at the back of the church.'

Without waiting for an answer she stood up and beckoned Reade to follow her. Reade did not move at first, he was not used to members of the public ordering him around, it was always the other way round. Helen looked back at Reade after taking a couple of steps. 'Come on, I'll show you.'

They went to the window that overlooked the rear of the church. She pointed to a dome-shaped mausoleum, once covered with gold. The double doors were made of imposing oak and even closed, gave the impression of strength. It was obvious that this building had not been erected recently, the carvings on the stones were crumbling with age and restoration work was needed to bring the edifice back to its former glory. Helen said, 'See that, it's the Campbell burial place. Only for the big bosses of course.'

'How on earth do you know all this?' Reade was impressed.

'Apart from the fact that I've lived in this area all my life, I was brought up in Kilmun. I have lived in Dunoon for the past twenty years but I still come back to this kirk, it's my own. There's a great big poster in the church car park, it tells you the whole history.' She noted with satisfaction that Reade flushed. It was obvious that none of these coppers had seen fit to read the poster, they were too interested in the present to bother reading about the past. 'Now, I don't know how it could possibly help you but maybe whoever did this knew about the legend and did a copycat,' she suggested.

'Anything is possible with murder I suppose,' muttered Reade. He turned to Helen and said, 'Thank you for that, it may be useful.'

They shook hands, Helen with a firm grip nearly crushing Reade's hand. It was only after she had left and closed the door behind her that Reade allowed himself the luxury of rubbing his sore hand.

'Sir,' said Morris, 'I've got something on the First Marquis and Eighth Earl of Argyll. Born 1607 — executed 1661. He was a bit of a lad, he opposed Charles I and he actually welcomed Cromwell to Edinburgh, but he didn't want anything to do with an invasion of England. He fought against the English, and only changed his mind after he was besieged in Inveraray Castle. He sat in Richard Cromwell's Parliament in 1659. He then changed sides and actually placed the crown on Charles II's head at Scone. Anyway, in 1660, once Charles II had settled in he presented himself at court. I expect he thought he would get some reward. He did all right, he was imprisoned, charged with treason since 1638 and an accessory to the death of Charles I. He was found guilty and executed.'

'I suppose your little computer told you,' said Reade in a voice dripping with sarcasm.

'No, Sir. There's a pamphlet here, once she mentioned it I looked it up, I could have gone onto the Internet and found it, but it is quicker to read a pamphlet.' Morris replied with no sign that he had heard the sarcasm in Reade's voice. Morris had recognised the tone of voice of course, he had to put up with sarcasm and more because of his nature and his preoccupation with computers, but he had found the best way to cope with it was to completely ignore it. It saved so much aggravation.

'It's very interesting but I hardly think that it has a bearing on this case. Now get on with what you are supposed to be doing.' Reade was irritated and out of sorts. This talk of the past disturbed him; he had no idea how such information could have any bearing on the present.

A car drove up outside. A tall man in his early fifties got out. He had dark hair liberally streaked with grey, and dressed in casual grey trousers with a turtle necked grey sweater. He had been an excellent athlete in his youth but lately he'd stopped training and his muscles had begun to sag a little. Reade glanced out of the window and recognised him as Detective Superintendent Frederick Thomson. 'Fiery Fred', his nickname, had been earned in his younger days. His temper was renowned throughout the Force. He cultivated this reputation: it had its advantages and helped keep his 'troops' in order.

Thomson had spent most of his service in the Criminal Investigation Department, but two years previously he had transferred to the uniform branch intending to enhance his career. He had been in uniform for just six weeks when he decided that he hated the internal politics: fighting tooth and nail with headquarters staff for money to police the streets instead of financing the latest crackpot idea someone had come up with at the place known as 'Fantasy Island'.

Quality of Service surveys, re-organisations, anything except keeping the streets safe. If he'd had one more meeting with the local neighbourhood watch he would have gone crazy. A vacancy occurred, unexpectedly, in CID for a Superintendent's job, just as he was thinking he would revert to Detective Chief Inspector to get out of the hole he had dug for himself. He jumped at the chance to move sideways. 'Fiery Fred' decided he would never again seek promotion if he had to leave the CID.

Detective Chief Inspector MacLeod had been filling the vacancy as Detective Superintendent whilst a decision was being made as to who should be offered the post. MacLeod hated the job: too much paperwork and too many hours tied to the desk in the working day. He made the same decision as Thomson; for similar reasons, he was a worker and realised that Detective Chief Inspector was the rank he wanted to keep. Any further promotions would make him very unhappy. He did not get on with administrators being blunt to the point of rudeness. The extra money was nice and his pension would be enhanced but he was quite prepared to give that up for job satisfaction. He was pleased he had found out before the promotion board and he consciously made the decision not to apply for promotion. He had to put up with colleagues and his senior officers nagging him to change his mind, but he was adamant, he would remain as he was and never go any further. He had a few years left to serve, perhaps he would change his mind in the future but he didn't think so.

Peter Reade inwardly groaned. First Helen MacDonald and now 'Fiery Fred' had turned up, it just wasn't his day. He said to Morris, 'The Detective Superintendent is here, get the kettle on.' He hoped that MacLeod would come back soon. Reade hated entertaining very senior officers; he could not make conversation easily and did not have the talent to make small talk when he felt uneasy. Thomson made him very uneasy indeed.

Both Reade and Morris stood up when Thomson entered the room. 'Sit down, don't stand on ceremony. Where's the Detective Chief Inspector?' Thomson waved his hand in the air and turned to Reade looking him full in the face. Reade opened his mouth and was about to answer when MacLeod and Milton walked into the room.

'Where's the car?' asked Thomson.

'No car, Sir, we walked,' said Milton.

'Walked!' Thomson exclaimed, putting the back of his hand to his forehead in mock shock. 'I feel faint, when was the last time you two walked anywhere?'

'We do walk sometimes you know!' said MacLeod.

'Especially when the house is only a couple of hundred yards away,' muttered Milton under his breath.

'I heard that.' MacLeod wheeled and gave Milton a friendly slap on the shoulder. 'Don't tell him all our secrets, now get the kettle on, I'd love a cup of coffee, I'm fed up with tea!' Milton smiled and busied himself at the table clattering the mugs.

'What brings you here?' MacLeod asked Thomson. 'You don't often call in.' ('On a Sunday, too' he thought but refrained from saying it out loud. He may have done so if they had been alone together, but not in front of junior officers. They had known each other long enough to permit such friendly banter between them.)

Thomson said, 'I know but I was passing, my mother lives in Dunoon at a home for the elderly, she loves it. My wife loves visiting too. I'm not sure, all those old people. They do line dancing, swimming and have classes for pottery, it makes me tired, and not a little disturbed.'

'Maybe because you see your own future?' MacLeod said. He could imagine Thomson doing line dancing and the vision made him nearly laugh out loud.

'Not a chance, I want a graceful old age if you don't mind. Slippers, TV and a little gardening. I can't be doing with their kind of 'retirement'. Enough of idle chit-chat. Update me.'

MacLeod indicated that they should go into the small anteroom, which he was using as an office cum conference room. They entered. The atmosphere in the main incident room visibly relaxed.

Thomson had no idea of the effect he had on his subordinates. They respected him, and some even liked him, but his reputation for his volcanic temper was universal. 'Walking on broken glass' was the best description of their attitude towards him, and most refused to even speak to him unless they had to. Others who knew him well, like MacLeod, knew that there was a pussycat inside 'Fiery Fred' and he actively cultivated his reputation so no-one would find out the real man. MacLeod told Thomson as much as they knew.

A short time later when Detective Inspector Janet MacBain and Detective Sergeant Susan Lampart arrived back from the autopsy, the office was unnaturally quiet. 'We're back,' said Susan to the team. She was bouncy and full of life, the post-mortem was over and she was relieved.

'Shh.' Peter Reade nodded his head towards the inner office. Just then the door opened and Thomson and MacLeod came out, Susan visibly blanched, she had crossed Thomson some time ago and hoped he had forgotten. He had, but she would never know it.

'You're happy considering you've just been to a post-mortem,' growled Thomson. 'What was said?'

Susan looked at MacLeod, he nodded his head. His staff were well trained to defer to him before telling anyone anything and that included the 'Boss'. She told them that the man had been strangled, then from a quarter of an hour to an hour later he was decapitated. The knife did the 'business'.

Janet handed the Detective Superintendent the knife that was in a clear plastic bag. She said, 'It looks like a machete to me, it may have been home made. I've never seen anything like it.'

'I have.' Thomson was sure. 'I was in the Army as a youngster and I've seen something like this, it's a bayonet machete. I was in the Artillery and there's a collection at Woolwich, or there was, the way the Army has changed now, no doubt someone has sold the collection to get money, they seem to always be broke now.'

'I was in the Army but I've never seen anything like this.' MacLeod picked up the bag carefully and looked at the knife. 'I would have thought it was home made, but if you say it's a Military weapon, then I'll agree with you. It's not British Army is it?'

'No. I can't remember where it comes from, but I know I've seen one,' said Thomson.

'Maybe the marking could tell us,' said Janet.

MacLeod peered closer and saw a faint mark stamped on the hilt. 'Missed that,' he thought. 'I'll get an appointment at the opticians as soon as I can, my eyesight isn't what it used to be.' He said aloud, 'Get it to forensic, they may be able to bring it up. We'll find out more then.'

'I'll try to find it on the Internet,' Morris said. He immediately wished he hadn't. All eyes turned to him, he hated being the centre of attention and he had now become the object of Detective Superintendent Thomson's gaze.

'Are you the computer expert, young man?' said Thomson.

'Yes,' squeaked Morris wishing the ground would swallow him up. 'Good, Mr MacLeod needs someone like you on his team, do it and tell me the results. I'll be thinking about it until I know, I hate half-remembering something.'

MacLeod frowned and sadly looked at young Morris. He will learn to speak to the Superintendent when spoken to, volunteering information was liable to get him into trouble. 'I'll sort it out,' Reade murmured to MacLeod. He knew exactly what MacLeod was thinking, the look on his face was enough.

'What did Mrs Stewart have to say?' Milton asked Janet to change the subject away from young Morris. Milton liked him and felt protective towards him, he always seemed to be on the verge of falling over his own feet, figuratively speaking, and needed someone to look after him.

'We have an appointment in an hour, she wanted to have lunch first. We are having a meal first too,' said Janet.

'Don't go to Black the Bakers, the home made meringues are no good for the figure,' Thomson said eyeing Janet's figure. She could only be described as pleasantly plump. Janet took no offence, she knew she had put on a little weight. Not having regular meals and snacking was her downfall. CID work is not a regular nine to five job and meals have to be fitted in whenever possible. She always had a packet of biscuits in the car to assuage hunger pangs. She would have to lose weight, but not just yet!

'That all right Sir, I think the meringues are safe. ['For now' she thought.] We are going back to Dunoon, to the Argyll Hotel. There's nothing much open on a Sunday and we are meeting Mrs Stewart there anyway.' She didn't like to tell Thomson that Black the Bakers was closed on a Sunday and she wouldn't be able to get a meringue anyway.

The telephone rang, and was answered by Detective Sergeant Milton. Thomson turned to MacLeod: 'I'd better get off now, my wife will be getting agitated. She probably thinks this murder is convenient to stop me spending the whole day with my mother. You have my mobile number. If there's anything I need to know ring me, I'll leave you alone now.' Thomson had hated being over supervised when he was a Detective Chief Inspector and liked to allow his staff as much freedom as possible to get on with the job. He trusted MacLeod and his team implicitly.

After Thomson swept out of the room, Milton said to MacLeod, 'That was WPC O'Neill. Mrs Campbell says that she is ready to see us.' MacLeod picked up his mobile phone and was about to leave when Morris 'accidentally' dropped the pamphlet he had been discussing with Detective Inspector Reade onto the floor at MacLeod's feet.

MacLeod picked it up and saw in bold print, 'The History of the Campbell Clan'. 'What's this?' he asked Morris. 'Oh! That's nothing really,' Detective Inspector Reade said quickly before Morris could answer. 'Helen MacDonald came in and told us about him. Apparently he was beheaded and she thought there might be some connection, as if anything that happened in the seventeenth century could have any connection. The only fact linking the two is that they were both decapitated.'

'Not the Wicked Witch of the West,' Milton laughed. 'Did you enjoy her visit.'

'Not really, but we have to listen to all sorts,' Peter glowered.

MacLeod finished reading the potted history of the First Marquis and said, 'A traitor to both sides I see, he swapped sides between Cromwell and the Crown quite often. Perhaps our intrepid reporter may have given us at least a motive. If we find whom he betrayed then maybe we'll find the killer. I can't think of another motive — yet . . . ' He paused. ' . . . But you are wrong, Peter, this man was hanged, therefore he was strangled, and so was our victim; two Campbells with centuries between them dying in a similar way, except one was illegal and the other legal.'

7

MacLeod and Milton arrived at the Revered Campbell's house some five minutes later. They had travelled by car; it was too far to walk from the incident room for comfort. As they walked up the path from the drive the dark stone walls topped by old big dark green holly bushes seemed to loom over them and cut out the bright sunlight of a glorious day. The house stood silent, matching the dark sombre mood of the path. Gravel crunched underfoot echoing in the silence of the day. They could hear little except for a small child shouting love of life in the distance with a swift sharp mother's voice that quickly silenced the youthful glee.

MacLeod shuddered and said to Milton, 'I know houses are not supposed to have souls but I get the feeling that this house has not been happy.'

'I know what you mean,' replied Milton. 'It's a lovely day, but this house could make you shiver at any time. I'm pleased we aren't visiting at night.'

WPC O'Neill opened the door, and seemed genuinely pleased to see them. 'Come in.

Julia — I mean Mrs Campbell is in the living room.' They picked their way carefully through the removal boxes in the hallway. The preparation for the move was well under way, but there was no air of expectation of a joyful move, just sadness. It seemed that the heart had been torn out of the house.

'James Balfour arrived about ten minutes ago, he is with her,' said WPC O'Neill.

'Who's he?' asked MacLeod.

'Oh, he is one of the church elders and a local lawyer. He came round to see if there was anything he could do, apparently the families are great friends,' replied O'Neill.

'Mrs Balfour didn't come with him,' Milton asked, more of a statement than a question. 'I asked him about that, apparently she is very upset and thought she would make matters worse if she couldn't control herself.'

'Does Mrs Campbell know that her husband's head is missing?' asked MacLeod. He hoped she knew, he didn't want to tell her about his mutilation.

'No, and I don't think she should be told as yet. I'll do it when the time is right, if that's all right with you, Sir.'

MacLeod was relieved, it was bad enough she had lost her husband, she would know when the time was right.

100

'Has she asked how he was murdered?' queried MacLeod.

'That's the funny thing, she hasn't. She has just accepted our word that he was murdered and doesn't seem to want to know if we suspect anyone or any details or anything. I think she is just accepting the death first. She will ask, and I'm prepared for the questions but if there is any information you want me to keep back, just say so,' replied O'Neill.

MacLeod thought for a moment and said, 'No there's nothing, what we know she should know at the moment.'

As they were about to go into the lounge WPC O'Neill stopped MacLeod and said, 'How long do I have to stay here?' She seemed anxious.

'Is there anything wrong?' asked MacLeod.

'Not really, but I don't like this house.'

'I know what you mean,' thought MacLeod but he said, 'You'll stay as long as it takes or until Mrs Campbell doesn't need you anymore.' With that they went into the living room.

Mrs Campbell was sitting in a large wing-backed chair next to an inglenook fireplace. The fireplace seemed to dominate the whole of the room, built of local stone capped with a heavy mahogany mantelpiece devoid of ornaments. A large gothic mirror hung menacingly over the mantelpiece. A fire had been lit in the hearth: Iain had decided that his mother needed warmth despite the warm day and the glow of the flames struggled to light the gloom of the house.

Mrs Campbell sat ramrod straight in the chair, her face was red and her eyes were swollen from crying. She stared straight ahead and allowed the tears to run freely down her cheeks. She clutched a fine linen handkerchief, occasionally dabbing at the flow.

Mr James Balfour sat on a sofa that was crammed into the window recess. He leant towards Julia, his hands clenched, the knuckles white. He appeared in total distress at the sight of his friend. In any other society he would have been allowed to cry, but he was a macho Scotsman: tears are not permitted, not in public anyway. He rose as the officers entered the room; and seemed to unfold from the sofa to stand at his full height of some six foot three inches. He was in his late forties, tall and slim, a typical Scot with sandy fair hair, fair skin and startling blue eyes. He introduced himself and MacLeod returned the compliment.

MacLeod introduced both himself and Milton to Mrs Campbell. She gazed up at them with watery eyes and shakily asked them to sit down. Julia was at that moment unsure whether her voice would hold out. Although she had assured Margaret O'Neill that she was ready and prepared to talk to the detectives, she wanted this over as soon as possible.

'Would you like a cup of tea?' she asked. MacLeod really did not want another cup of anything to drink but it always put people at ease if their hospitality was accepted. WPC O'Neill decided that it would be appropriate if she left to make it. She would stay out as long as she could to allow Detective Chief Inspector MacLeod and Detective Sergeant Milton time to question Mrs Campbell without another person in the room to make it overcrowded, thus allowing Julia space to relax.

James Balfour said, 'I'm here as a family friend rather than a lawyer, I came to pay my respects and find out if there is anything I can do. We have been friends for many years now and I am totally shocked . . . ' He trailed off. 'Sorry. You came to see Julia. Do you want me to stay Julia?' He turned to her and put a comforting hand on her shoulder.

'No James, you get back to Fran, she needs you.' Mrs Campbell got up, took hold of his hands and gently guided him to the door.

It appeared akin to the child being removed from adult company and Balfour left without further protest.

MacLeod was somewhat relieved. He liked lawyers on the whole, but he did not know this one and preferred to conduct his business in private. Iain Campbell came into the room; he had been in his bedroom when the detectives had arrived. He had been lying on his bed thinking how different everything had been a mere week ago when he had been in Glasgow in the rooms he shared with three others. In fact he had been in bed at this time without a care in the world, now his world had turned upside down and would never be the same again. He heard the detectives in the lounge with his mother and debated whether or not he should stay away but then he thought of his mother's distress and decided he should be with her at this time. She looked so vulnerable and needed him and his father would have wanted it.

'Are you ready for this, Mum?' She nodded. 'Are you sure?' he said. He felt it was his duty to protect her from the outside world. He felt angry, sad, vulnerable and totally disorientated. He knew he had to put his feelings aside to help his mother, or at least try.

'Yes, now go away. I need to talk to these

gentlemen and I need to do it now.' She tried to be gentle with him, but she did not want him present. He should at least keep the illusion that she was happy with his father and she felt that she might say something Iain would not understand. 'Take my car and go see Ewen, it will do you good to get out for a while.'

Iain glared at MacLeod and Milton, but did as his mother asked. He said as he left the room, 'All right, but I won't be long,' and left closing the door quietly behind him.

Julia turned to MacLeod and said quietly, 'What do you want to know?'

MacLeod looked at Mrs Campbell and sensed that she was holding herself together by an act of will, but he also sensed something else in her, steel in her character perhaps? She had fallen apart and was now putting herself together. He was also pleasantly surprised, in the space of a few hours he had met two sons who were protective of their mothers, which made his day. The usual youths he met in the normal routine work had no sense of respect for anyone, least of all their own mothers.

'We can come back later if you wish,' MacLeod half rose from his seat. Julia put her hand up to stop him.

'No, we must get on with it.'

'When did you last see your husband?' MacLeod asked.

Julia replied, 'About six o'clock last night.' She paused as if visualising him and her eyes filled up. 'He went out, he didn't say where he was going. I thought he was visiting a member of the congregation. I presumed it was Mrs Graham, she has just come out of hospital and he had been visiting her recently. She has had a cancer operation and is having a hard time.' MacLeod was usually reluctant to interrupt but he sensed that Julia was about to regale them with a detailed explanation of Mrs Graham's illness.

'Didn't you worry when he failed to return home?'

Julia thought about the question for a moment. She could not tell these men they were not sleeping together, that they had been in separate bedrooms for many years. They looked like solid happy husbands and would not understand, after all she hardly understood it herself. 'Not really, he often stayed out all night with someone who needed him.' For the first time Julia looked at MacLeod properly. 'He was a good pastor to his flock, but he tended to forget I worried. After twenty-five years of marriage I got used to it. I suppose your wife is the same.'

MacLeod was taken aback. This woman looked at him with startling blue eyes and they seemed to penetrate his soul. It was as if she knew exactly what he was thinking. He cleared his throat and glanced away. 'I try to ring her when I can, usually once a day when I'm away, but it can be difficult. She understands.'

Julia said, 'Yes, and I understand, only too well.' She allowed a hint of bitterness to creep into her voice.

Milton saw that MacLeod was shaken by this exchange. All police officers are acutely aware of the lack of time they spend with their own families. They do not like to be reminded of the sacrifices they have to make to do their job. Milton asked, 'Why would he be in the kirk at that time of night?'

Julia turned to him and said, 'He was always there when there was an important service the next day. A wedding, Easter, Christmas and always before a Christening or funeral.'

Milton asked, 'Was this well known?'

'I should think so, it wasn't a secret,' Julia replied.

Whilst Milton was talking to Mrs Campbell MacLeod watched her intently; she was getting stronger by the minute, or so it seemed. Milton continued, 'Can you

107

remember anything unusual happening over the last few days?'

Julia said, 'No nothing at all, we've been packing if you can call that unusual, but no, nothing else.'

MacLeod decided that it was his turn to take over the questioning. 'Did he have any enemies?' he asked.

'I should imagine so, but I couldn't tell you who they were.' Julia was perplexed, what a question to ask about a minister.

As if to himself MacLeod said, 'Why would anyone want to do that to him?' He then realised she did not know about the decapitation and was pleased that she did not ask what 'that' may be and she continued with her answers.

'I suppose for a number of reasons, after all no-one is a saint and we all make enemies. Even you Mr MacLeod, but in your line of business I should say especially you.' Julia realised she may have said too much and was about to reveal things about her marriage best left unsaid. 'Now I'm feeling a little weak so if you don't mind I want to have a rest.' She sank back into the chair and looked at the fire, watching the flames leap into the dark sooty lum.

WPC O'Neill came into the room with a tray of tea and biscuits. She looked with concern at Julia and placed the tray on the small coffee table adjacent to Julia's chair.

'Perhaps you could continue this later Sir, I think Mrs Campbell has had enough. Do you want a cup of tea before you go?'

MacLeod declined the offer with thanks and decided to continue with any questioning later.

When MacLeod and Milton went outside, MacLeod glanced back to the sandstone house. 'I still find that house oppressive.'

'Maybe it's the occupants, not the house,' suggested Milton. They got into the car. Before they could move off a small green mini came out of the garage from the side of the house and was driven at high speed out of the driveway and up the road. 'Iain didn't leave straight away. I wonder where he was eavesdropping from?'

'I expect from the window, I thought I saw a shadow,' Milton observed. 'Ah well! I suppose I would have been the same if my mother was being interviewed by the police.'

MacLeod was not concerned about this incident. He had no objection to Iain listening to the conversation, it had been his mother who hadn't wanted him present. In his investigations he liked to see the close family either all together or as soon as possible one after the other, after all most murders are committed by relatives or close friends of the victim. He would never jump to conclusions, and fit the facts to convict a suspect, he would rather ten guilty persons go free than one innocent be convicted.

Milton interrupted his train of thought: 'A strong lady, but a little weird.'

'Yes, and we will have to go back. She isn't ready to talk properly but she wouldn't have said anything else. She can't be pushed too hard. She is brittle and could break, I don't want a breakdown on my conscience.' MacLeod could be insensitive sometimes, but he knew it would attract severe criticism if he was overbearing with an innocent spouse of the victim and caused a mental problem.

'Why didn't you ask about them sleeping apart?' asked Milton. 'Not yet. I want to keep that up my sleeve for the moment. She may or may not have anything to do with the murder and I want some leverage. We know her husband has betrayed her and she is a strong woman in all senses of the word. She's on the list of suspects.'

'What number?' asked Milton.

'In the first three,' MacLeod replied without hesitation.

8

Detective Sergeant John Milton parked the car in a lay-by overlooking the Clyde towards Greenock. Detective Chief Inspector Cameron MacLeod could almost see his house. His tummy rumbled. 'I'm hungry and Morag is making Sunday lunch for the girls.' He sighed: 'Roast beef, fluffy Yorkshire puddings, roast potatoes and,' he gave a further sigh, 'gorgeous onion gravy.'

Milton reached into the back of the car and handed MacLeod a cheese sandwich, clinically wrapped in stiff plastic, overpriced, overlong in the tooth and definitely lacking in taste. MacLeod first looked at the sandwich and then gave Milton a pained stare.

'Perhaps I should have organised a proper lunch, maybe you would be in a better mood then.'

'I'm not in a bad mood,' said MacLeod as he snatched the sandwich from Milton. 'I'm just hungry and I hate murder enquiries, you know that.'

'Whatever you say,' said Milton, 'but next time we eat out.'

They sat in silence and gazed at the deep

blue water reflecting an azure blue sky. Small white sailing boats glided effortlessly past. MacLeod liked to have time to reflect on any interview; he subconsciously noted things that did not surface until later. This was his time to think. Until now he had been too busy to really think. He visualised the murderer; he or she must have waited for Campbell in the kirk, but why such an hour? Or did Campbell make an appointment with his killer? He thought about the actual murder. Was it committed in the graveyard, or the kirk? If in the graveyard then what possessed Campbell to accompany the perpetrator? Perhaps he had been knocked unconscious in the kirk then carried out, if so it must have taken some strength. 'No,' thought MacLeod, 'he went willingly or was persuaded to go to his place of death. He was certainly killed in the kirk. Forensic evidence would surely bear this out.'

'Have we checked the kirk, John?' he said aloud.

'Aye, that we have. There's nothing out of the ordinary as far as we can tell. Forensic went over it with a fine tooth comb,' said Milton. Milton was used to these silences and then unconnected questions out of the blue. It was how MacLeod worked. Sometimes nothing pleased him, then suddenly for no reason he would become affable. The change of mood usually preceded a solution to whatever problem was on his mind. Milton had known MacLeod too many years to take any offence. There was another deep silence.

MacLeod's active brain was again working. He wondered about the way Campbell was killed, it was not so very unusual, but the mutilation of the body certainly was. Perhaps the murderer was trying to tell him something. If it was connected with the turncoat Marquis who suffered beheading because he was a traitor then it was like taking a sledgehammer to crack a nut — very unsophisticated. For someone to mutilate a body shows that there was a great deal of emotion involved in the killing, it was almost an act of vengeance, or the killer was a psychopath perhaps? Now where was the head? A trophy hunter? — no, that was ridiculous; maybe someone unconnected with the local area, a violent stranger?

'Have we checked to see if any other ministers have been murdered, John?'

Milton thought, 'So that's where he's going, a serial killer perhaps?'

'No, but I'll get someone on to it. I still think it's a local. I'll check if there have been any strangers in the village. It's not a popular area for tourists to stay; they normally come here for a few hours then move on. I think we will be told by the locals if anyone strange is around.'

'Now, where is the head? I find it horrific somehow that it was taken. It couldn't stop his identification, after all Sergeant Gillespie recognised him, and identification papers were left in his wallet.'

'Maybe a Black Magic ritual,' said Milton, more as a thought out loud rather than a serious question.

MacLeod nearly choked on his sandwich. 'Don't be ridiculous,' he snapped, 'there's nothing like that here, and I don't want any suggestion of it when we get back. Foolish talk like that can divert an investigation from its proper path.'

'I didn't mean it like that, I was only speculating. Don't get out of sorts,' said Milton.

MacLeod muttered, 'I'm not out of sorts. But I hate any mention of that sort of thing.'

'Perhaps you believe in it?' Milton posed an uncomfortable question to MacLeod.

'Not a chance,' came back the immediate reply. 'I don't believe in anything I can't feel, touch or smell. Now can we please change the subject, and take me back to the incident room.'

Milton nodded and started the car; he glanced at MacLeod with a smile on his lips. He had been too long on this earth not to know that there were some things he could not explain. Although in this case he agreed with MacLeod he felt there was a more earthly reason for the murder. He enjoyed winding up his boss, sometimes he pricked him into thinking laterally and it bore fruit.

Both MacLeod and Milton would have been envious of the two women detectives who were elsewhere, comfortable, having had an ample sufficiency of good food. Janet MacBain and Susan Lampart were sitting in the lounge bar of the Argyll Hotel in Dunoon, looking out towards the Caledonian MacBrayne Ferry point. The Pioneer was docking and they were fascinated at the smooth precision with which the boat was berthed at the pier. It came in over the flat blue water causing a ripple of white foam, and seemed to approach the pier too fast as if it were never going to stop, then suddenly turned hard to the left and smoothly settled gently against the ancient wooden struts of the pier. 'One day it won't stop,' thought Janet, 'and I hope I am here to see it. Now wouldn't that be fun.'

It was getting quite late in the afternoon.

Mrs Stewart was late for their appointment. They had eaten well, enjoying the steak pie for which the Argyll was rightly proud, with all the trimmings, plus peas as a treat; it was a rarity when peas were on the menu. Mrs White, one of the proprietors of the hotel, did not approve of having the same vegetables on the menu every day. She didn't like peas herself and it was an exceptional day indeed when she put them on the menu.

'Do you think we have time for a speciality ice cream?' Janet was studying the menu. 'This one is death by chocolate in any other form. Look, butterscotch, scoops of chocolate ice cream topped with cream and whipped cream, Oh! Heaven.'

She was almost drooling. 'No way, you told me not to let you have an ice cream. Think of the diet, you would have to starve for a week after one of those,' said Susan.

'What! I'll have to pull rank here. I know what I said but I have the will power of a gnat where food is concerned.' Janet was nothing if not honest.

'Men too!' Susan was prying gently; she knew little of Janet's private life even though they had worked together for years. She knew through the 'grapevine' that Janet had had a long-term relationship with a married colleague and that they had recently parted.

116

Janet's usual reaction to emotional turmoil had always been to overeat, and Susan noticed Janet had been overeating with a vengeance. She tried to get Janet to talk about it, to little effect, and the reply she was given was frosty.

'Off limits, Susan, I'm only weak for food.' Janet had a pang of both pleasure and pain as a brief vision of her ex-lover surfaced. She knew she had done the right thing some months ago when she finished with him. He had given all the usual lies for years, 'I'll leave her', 'I love only you', and all that crap. She had believed him, all his empty promises. Now he had someone else and just last week he had the nerve to ring her to say he had left his empty marriage to live with his new love. 'I didn't want to lose her like I lost you.' The words rang in her ears together with raging anger at her own stupidity.

Fortunately the conversation was abruptly terminated when Mrs White bustled to their table. 'Mrs Stewart is here. I'm sure you would like to use the back bar, I've put your coffee there.' Mrs White knew these two detectives and she preferred her customers to enjoy themselves without being disturbed by overhearing unpleasant conversations. Murder was not for *her* lounge.

They went through to the back bar where Mrs Stewart was comfortably sitting pouring herself a cup of coffee. There was a full pot of coffee on a tray with three cups, a milk jug and a plate of biscuits, which Janet was eyeing with longing. She had what is known as a healthy appetite and the recent reminder of 'Dave-the-Bastard' didn't help. Introductions were made and they asked if they could use first names; it was friendlier and neither detective stood on ceremony, nor were they rank conscious.

'Well Maureen, we have been told that you may know something about the Reverend William Campbell, what can you tell us?' said Janet.

'Yes, I certainly do.' Maureen was flattered that she would be able to help. She knew very well that it was either her boss, Duncan Grey, or maybe that reprobate Detective Chief Inspector Cameron MacLeod who had directed these two officers to her. She wasn't put out at all, she liked a good gossip and she was about to have one with a vengeance. If she could find out any details from the girls she would. It would satisfy her soul to know something no-one else knew, apart from the police that is. She could keep a secret if asked, but people rarely asked. When they did she was sorely disappointed

118

but was honourable enough to abide by their wishes.

She sat back in the easy chair with a coffee in her hand and said to Janet and Susan, 'What do you want to know about William Campbell?'

'First, what was the Reverend Campbell like as a person?' asked Janet.

'I thought he was a weak man, not that I disliked him, you understand. I'm upset that he is dead, but over the years I have heard things now and then. He loved women and some of them loved him too. He gave the appearance of being happily married.' Her voice dropped and she became conspiratorial as if someone could overhear them. 'But he couldn't have been or why would he have strayed? My theory is that he liked to have his cake and eat it.'

Janet nodded her head in agreement but she was not thinking only of Campbell, another intruded into her mind. 'Was this well known?' she asked.

'Oh, no!' Maureen was emphatic. 'It's only because I know personally some of his women friends, that I can tell you anything at all.'

Janet gave Maureen an old-fashioned look and said, 'You haven't told us any facts yet.'

'Be patient, I'll get to that,' replied Maureen. 'The Very Reverend William Campbell came to Kilmun some fifteen or so years ago from Glasgow. Even then there were some rumours. There was something in his past but it's so long ago I really can't remember what it was. Anyway, he settled down here and it was quite a while before there were any rumours about him.' Susan sighed a little. Maureen liked to hear the sound of her own voice.

Maureen heard the sigh and realised she was rambling a bit. She continued: 'Now you must understand that there has been no proof of his infidelities. I only have someone's word for it. He has never been seen with any other woman so it could be their vivid imagination.'

'That's all right,' said Janet. 'Most of our work is rumour and imagination, we have to get proof for Court, but every little helps.'

Maureen relaxed a little and said, 'Fine, he usually went for lonely widows or divorcees who appreciated his attentions. I could name at least five. Perhaps there were more, but I only know of five. His wife apparently knew all about them, she isn't a stupid woman. I don't think he ever, as far as I know, had an affair with a woman who was married and still living with her partner.

Susan asked, 'Are there any jealous new husbands or boyfriends about? You never know. The murderer seems to have been in some frenzy.'

Maureen's eyes lit up. She was about to find something out, but Janet interrupted and said, 'Go on with your tale.'

Maureen sighed and said, 'Not that I know of, the ladies that I have mentioned were always alone, and mostly of similar age to him. He didn't seem to go for the younger woman. He liked maturity in a woman.'

'Who was the latest one?' asked Janet.

'Mrs Jones, the receptionist at the doctor's surgery in Kilmun is the last one I know about.' Maureen paused. 'But I've been told that this has finished and he has found someone else. I don't know who the 'someone else' is.' There was definite regret in her voice now. 'He was faithful in a way to his mistresses, he never took one on without first stopping the relationship with the other.'

Janet's eyebrows shot up, she thought that Maureen hadn't realised what she had said. Campbell was dreadfully unfaithful to his wife and family and seemed to have used these unfortunate women, preying on them when they were most vulnerable. Her own recent experience with such a 'love-rat' had

121

coloured her emotions; she knew this, but no amount of telling herself that she was experiencing an irrational reaction could stop the anger at this Irreverent Gentleman rising in her throat and almost choking her.

She heard Maureen say, 'He was a good minister and no-one wanted him to leave.'

Janet was dumbfounded. Susan saw that her colleague was struggling with herself and decided to ask the next question: 'How do you know all this?' Susan was amazed that this small community tolerated a minister with the obvious morals of an alley cat. Janet was not surprised, after having bitter experience with such a charmer, 'Perhaps he thought he was doing the women a favour,' she thought. Whenever such a man was found out, all the sympathy was for him, not the women he had hoodwinked.

Maureen replied, 'Oh, from this and that, here and there. Mostly I listen and people talk to me. I don't suppose they know it all. I know I don't know it all, but I don't think I've left anything out. I do know he had affairs with 'single' women, which made the married women content. These women didn't go after the husbands and the fact that he didn't mess with married women made their husbands content. I heard someone say he was doing a public service.'

'Some service.' Janet was quite horrified.

'I don't know, he didn't hurt anyone,' said Susan.

'What about his wife, she was the loser.' Janet had not thought about her Dave's wife whilst they were seeing each other. It wasn't as if she was uncaring but he told her that he didn't have a marriage as such, they slept in separate bedrooms. What he didn't tell her was that he only used the spare bedroom when he was on night shift because it was quieter and he could get some sleep.

'Yes, I suppose so.'

'Though she still had him at home,' said Susan.

Maureen thought about her own husband at home, sleeping in the chair, she tried to imagine what it would be like not to know what he was doing when he went out. Her husband was a member of the Bowl's Club and in the winter he, like a good number of Dunoon residents, stayed at home rather than go out. Home was comfortable. 'I think I would rather not have him at home if he was out with other women,' she said.

'How do you know he was having extra-marital relations with them?' said Susan. 'Perhaps it was only friendship.'

The look on Maureen's and Janet's faces said, 'How naive can you get?' Janet forced a smile and said, 'Perhaps you are right, the only way we are going to find out is to see these women. Can you tell us who they are, Maureen?'

'I could but I won't, I've given you one name and I was hoping we could keep the others out of it, they are all my friends you know.' She saw the disappointment on Janet's face. 'Well, ask Mr MacLeod if it's necessary, if it is I'll give you their names but at least two have re-married so please be discreet.'

It was only later when Maureen was at home watching her husband sleeping in his chair that she realised she hadn't learned a thing from the two detectives, though they had obtained a lot from her. More than she had really intended. Never mind, she would learn all she needed to know and more once she went into work. Being the Fiscal's secretary had its advantages.

9

Detective Constable Morris was doing what he did best, sitting down, his computer fingers flying, getting Mr William Campbell's full history. Campbell had been born in Northern Ireland in 1949 of Protestant parentage. His father had served in the British Army during the war. He was demobbed as soon as he could get out, but like many others in his desperation to get home he had agreed to serve for five years reserve rather than serve for a couple more months. He did not believe that another war could erupt within those five years. How wrong he was, he was called up for Korea, although this was called a 'police action' rather than a war. After going through the Second World War without a scratch he had stepped on a land mine and was killed instantly.

Young William lost his father and then almost immediately lost his mother. His mother had a mental breakdown from which she never recovered. Young William was found wandering in the streets and his mother had to be committed to a mental hospital where she died in 1970. The death certificate said natural causes but there was a whiff of a possibility that she may have, at last, committed suicide. There were several attempts noted on her records at the hospital.

His Aunt Betty and Uncle Ross took William to Glasgow when his mother had gone into hospital. He had six cousins, all older than him. It was not known from records whether he ever visited his mother in hospital. A bright boy at school, William could have chosen to be anything in his life, but at the age of fifteen he decided to become a minister and all his efforts were directed to that goal. He trained at St Andrews University and met his wife there. It appears that she was pregnant almost immediately after their marriage. She had what is termed 'a honeymoon baby'.

Julia, his wife, trained as a chemist, but was never employed after her graduation. They had four children in all. Julia Campbell's sole employment became wife and mother, also unpaid secretary for her husband.

Morris gave the information to Detective Inspector Reade and said, 'I'll try to identify that knife. There may be information on the Internet, if there isn't then I could leave a query on a specialist Web-site and wait for a reply.'

Detective Inspector Reade looked up from

the pile of *proformas*, the results of the house to house inquiry that he was working on. He did not normally do the mundane task of crossing off the completed forms from the local electoral register. As he was not computer literate and as Detective Constable MacPherson was not in, he was the only one left to do the mundane work. He resented MacLeod allowing MacPherson time off. It interfered with his 'proper' work. He hated having to do work which was not commensurate with his rank, but MacLeod's team had to work together. If MacLeod had been the only one left he would have mucked in. 'No, don't leave a message, we don't want to appear foolish, but you can try to find what's there. Hope you have something else for MacLeod when he comes back,' he growled. 'This isn't good enough. I thought the Internet was all singing and dancing.'

Everything was there. Morris knew that Detective Inspector Reade was almost computer illiterate, like some more of the team he could mention, and trying to explain how the Internet worked was an impossible task. He decided to get on with the job in hand and turned to the screen. It would be harder now to get what Mr MacLeod wanted. He did not disobey the order to send out a question into 'cyberspace' and get a reply, but set up a search with the harder task of filtering out the information he didn't want.

At five thirty the team congregated in the incident room. Detective Chief Inspector MacLeod looked round the room. 'All here, hands up those who are missing,' quipped Milton. There was a murmur of laughter from the team.

'OK, settle down,' said MacLeod, 'What do we know up to now?'

'Well,' said Reade, 'I've collated what I can. The house to house hasn't produced anything useful yet.'

'We have interviewed Mrs Stewart, she says that she knows of five other women that Campbell had relationships with but she won't give us the names without your say-so. Please could you persuade her? Tell her we will be discreet,' said Janet.

'I'll get onto the Fiscal, he'll persuade her to give more information. If she doesn't then I'm afraid she'll have to accept what's coming to her.'

Milton turned to MacLeod and said, his tone indicated the shock he felt. 'You wouldn't arrest her?'

'Yes I would. She has information we need and if all else fails . . . ' He didn't finish the sentence. MacLeod turned to the rest of the

128

team and said, 'We have done enough for today. I doubt if we can do anything else. The murderer, if he is an outsider, will be well away.'

'I've arranged for a police constable to stay here and look after the room overnight, he will take messages if anyone rings or comes in,' said Reade.

'Who is going to pay for that?' asked MacLeod. The short time he spent as Acting Detective Superintendent had shown him the need for economy, if nothing else.

'It's OK, not us. It's been sorted through uniform and as he's not on overtime it won't cost any extra.'

'That's about it, we'll have to get away for the ferries. You know what it's like at this time of year. All of you have a good night's rest ready for tomorrow. I'll meet you at the car, Sergeant Milton, you can give me a lift back to the ferry to pick up my car.'

He walked to the door and stopped at the computer station. 'Come on Morris, that's enough.' MacLeod tapped him on the shoulder. 'What are you doing anyway?'

'I'm trying to find the knife. Where it comes from and where it could be found, but I'm not having much success.' Morris sounded gloomy. 'Perhaps forensic will come up with something. Now switch that thing off and go home to your lovely bride.'

Janet and Susan decided to drive home to Glasgow. Musing over the events of the day, they walked down the path of the church towards the car park. 'I wonder about the minister, he was a randy 'Old Tom',' said Janet. Her anger had completely faded and she was now in 'professional mode' where emotions get in the way of investigations. She usually only allowed herself the luxury of showing her anger or frustration or even pity when the case was over. Too many mistakes could be made when emotions clouded judgement.

'He wasn't that well endowed, I mean . . . ' Susan stuttered, 'Well you know what I mean.' Susan disliked talking about body parts; she even hated 'blue' jokes.

'It isn't what you've got, but how you use it,' Janet giggled, then remembered how much Susan got embarrassed at such things and said, 'We shouldn't be talking about him like this. I wonder where the head is.' A change of subject was definitely in order. 'When we find that I think we'll find the murderer.'

They walked in silence, each preoccupied with their own thoughts. Janet looked at Susan and felt she had more than this murder on her mind. 'How's things back

130

home?' Janet had noticed that Susan was not as chirpy as usual. The last few days she had been a little short tempered and less tolerant.

'Not so good, Jo has been very tired lately and I finally got her to go to the doctor's.' Susan looked about to cry.

'Sorry, I shouldn't have asked.' Janet put her hand out to touch Susan but changed her mind.

'No it's OK. I need someone to talk to. I have to be so bright at home. She's got cancer and the doctors aren't hopeful. When we found out, Jo was more supportive to me really. She's in hospital at the moment waiting for test results.' Susan said everything in a rush. She had no-one else to talk to whom she trusted and was relieved that Janet had asked her.

Janet put her hand on Susan's shoulder. She wanted to hug her but didn't want Susan to get the wrong idea. Although she knew she was definitely heterosexual, Susan wasn't and she wanted no ambiguity. 'Strange,' she thought, 'I would have no qualms about holding any other woman who was heterosexual, but not someone I know to be a lesbian.'

MacLeod was suddenly behind them, they were so engrossed in their mutual misery, one sympathetic the other deep in thought, that they hadn't heard him. 'Is everything all right?'

'Don't do that,' Janet exclaimed. 'Whistle or something. It doesn't do my heart any good when someone creeps up on me.'

'Sorry but I thought you heard me,' MacLeod said.

Before he could pursue his curiosity as to why his two female detectives were so upset Detective Sergeant Milton leant over the wall of the car park. 'Mr MacLeod, telephone for you, URGENT. It's the Detective Superintendent.'

MacLeod said to Janet and Susan. 'Hang on, we'll have a chat before you go.' He was always there for his staff whether they wanted to talk or not. If they were unhappy he didn't get the best out of them. It was selfish of him in a way; a happy team meant a good result. Misery always bred misery and lack of concentration on the job in hand.

* * *

Ewen Jones and Iain Campbell were sitting on the shore of Loch Eck near the Coylet Inn. Iain had left his home after MacLeod and Milton had started talking to his mother. He was upset about his father's death and now his mother had told him to get out. He went to Ewen, his friend and at once they had headed for the Coylet Inn. Iain needed a drink and arrived just in time to have one before the Coylet closed for the afternoon.

'I forgot it was Sunday Ewen, we should have gone somewhere else.'

'No matter, it's probably just as well, or we would have got drunk.' Ewen picked up a stone and threw it into the loch. 'Mum's in a state.'

'So is mine and she told me to get out. She said she needed to be alone. What do you think we should do?' said Iain.

Ewen thought for a moment and said, 'I think we should go back to Glasgow, but we have to stay. Our mothers need us.'

'But I need to get away, I need to get out of here,' said Iain.

'We can't and that's that.' Ewen was forceful. 'Don't worry, I'll look after you.' He put his arm round Iain who put his head on Ewen's shoulder and began to cry. Ewen had deliberately not asked Iain how he felt. He remembered how everyone had continually asked him how he felt when his father had left them. It made him feel worse. Iain would talk about his father when the time was right. It wasn't right now, Iain was too shaken up and his feelings were too raw.

They were both in shock at the moment.

Ewen and Iain had been friends from childhood, ever since Iain had come to Kilmun. Iain had stood by Ewen when his father had left and now it was Iain's turn to be supported.

'I hate having these coppers around Ewen, I think we could be in trouble.'

'Don't say anything.' Ewen put his hands on Iain's shoulders and made him turn to face him. 'We haven't done anything wrong. Not really wrong. Now promise me you will keep quiet.'

Iain looked a little frightened but nodded. Tears were falling down his face, an overwhelming sense of pity overtook Ewen and he held Iain close to him.

Ewen thought back to the day he had found his father in bed with another woman. He had been sent home from school early because he was unwell. He was only thirteen, but understood that what his father was doing was wrong. His father didn't know he had been seen and he couldn't tell his mother. He had run out of the house and waited until the woman had left before going back. He had recognised the woman; she was the lady who lived three doors away. He didn't know what to do or say and when he had plucked up the courage to tackle his father he was gone! One day he was there, the next gone and his mother spent most of her time crying.

Ewen ran to the only person he could trust, his best friend, Iain, the day his father had left home. He couldn't stand to see his mother crying. Mr Campbell had been at the door when he ran up to the Manse and had welcomed him as if he were a second son. He felt safe there. Ewen and Iain sat for a long time on the edge of the Loch, their companionship palpable with no need to talk.

★ ★ ★

Some six miles up the Loch at Jubilee Point Charlie Steele sat in his old mini car. He was a small but wiry man of exactly 55 years of age and was eagerly waiting for what he hoped would be a very profitable rendezvous. Charlie had been in the graveyard last night. He had forgotten to lock the hall and had hopped over the wall between Benmore Gardens and the kirk grounds. He wasn't suppose to use this as a short cut but no-one would see him and he felt the dead wouldn't mind. Just as he got to the last row of graves he saw a figure enter the side door of the kirk. When he recognised who it was he wondered why he should be going into the kirk at such an hour. Charlie had shrugged his shoulders, 'none of my business,' he had thought and after locking the hall had gone home.

The next day was a great shock to him when the minister's body had been found and he considered telling the police what he had seen, but changed his mind almost immediately. This was too good a chance to miss. One telephone call later proved that his decision to keep quiet had been the right one. It could prove to be a little pot of gold at the end of his own particular rainbow.

Charlie licked his lips at the thought of the money he would squeeze and squeeze. It was like winning the lottery. He would get a new car for a start, and he would get a few more clothes. He would have to be careful, after all he was on Benefit and any extra spending would be looked at. He didn't want to lose his Benefits, they knew he looked after the church hall but he only got £10 a week, so that didn't affect his money. Charlie mainly looked after the keys and did some odd jobs. The church was not rich and the only other person employed was the cleaner and she only worked twenty hours a week.

Totally absorbed in his thoughts, Charlie looked at the mountain and its reflection in the almost black water. Loch Eck is one of the deepest lochs in Scotland and the echo of the mountains is almost perfect when the day is calm and the sun shines in the right direction.

A tape of Boney M was playing in the car's radio-cassette machine. Charlie had been a fan for many years, following the group as soon as he heard them in his youth at a time when he thought that anything was possible. He liked to play his tapes when he was in a good mood. When he felt down and the music only reminded him of what might have been and made him more depressed, the tapes were consigned to the box and forgotten for a while. Charlie was no depressive personality and the music was not forgotten for long.

Charlie was singing slightly off key his version of 'Ra Ra Rasputin, lover of the Russian Queen' pretending he was the fifth member of the group, when he felt the passenger door open and he turned to see his new source of income. As he did so a large spanner was violently smacked into his face. Blood spurted, and he feebly put his hands forward to protect himself. He had no time to speak and lapsed into unconsciousness. He did not see the hand brake taken off, nor sense the car being pushed forward and slide under the dark waters of the Loch with virtually no sound at all. The car filled up and slowly sank under the dark waters. Air bubbled out from the car in plops, causing great ripples on the surface of the Loch, which gradually flowed to the other bank.

Unfortunately for the murderer the Loch was not as deep at this point as it was elsewhere and the mini settled on a shelf some fifteen feet from the surface. A few feet further up the Loch and the car would have gone down, never to be seen again.

One man's misfortune is another man's luck, or perhaps it was not Charlie's fate to disappear forever. About an hour later a rowing boat with two fishermen aboard appeared round the spit of land. They had taken a good catch of salmon, and were feeling full of the joys of spring.

As they dragged their craft to land one of them spotted the mini and saw Charlie's face that had been damaged beyond recognition. They grabbed their mobile phone and rang the police. Charlie was saved from the nibbles of the fish; his body was recovered.

10

In the incident room MacLeod picked up the telephone to speak to the Detective Superintendent. He hoped that this was a really urgent message and not a complete waste of time. He knew Detective Superintendent Thomson of old, who had a slight tendency to overreact to situations. 'Yes Sir, what can I do for you,' MacLeod said with forced interest in his voice.

'Cameron, you know my mother has lived in this area for many years, in fact she lived in Strone until a couple of years ago. She knows all about your corpse. News travels fast, she knew about the murder before I got here, anyway she's told me quite a bit about him. In brief, he was a popular man but she did not take to him. She felt he was too fond of the ladies. Now she also told me she had no proof of this. Just a feeling. We all know of randy ministers, but there was some talk that he had pressed his advances too far on one lady and she complained; it was all hushed up. The husband caught them and the lady cried rape. I hope she is wrong.'

MacLeod felt his heart sink. He had

just come to terms with Campbell being an inveterate womaniser, now there was the added complication of his being the one thing MacLeod actively hated, a rapist. Second only to child molesters, a man who forced himself on a woman was, in his view, sub-human. 'I do hope she is wrong too, it's probably an exaggeration. Do you mind if I keep the team on duty for another couple of hours? Will your budget stand it?' queried MacLeod.

'It will have to. Anyway, the Reverend Campbell was a respected member of the community and this case will attract more than passing interest when the press get hold of it. I want a result soon, as fast as you can, within twenty-four hours if possible. So no time off for anyone until it's done,' replied Thompson.

'Fine, but I will send the team off duty at eight o'clock. I would rather they were fresh in the morning. We will do what we can then.'

MacLeod put the phone down and sighed. He didn't like this and he would now have to tell the team. Fortunately no-one had left to go home. He gathered them in the incident room. 'Detective Superintendent Thomson wants a result. He has received information that Mr Campbell may have been accused of rape and it was hushed up.' MacLeod paused, then said between clenched teeth, 'He also said that there's no time off for anyone until this case is solved. Morris, find out if Campbell has any convictions for any kind of sexual assault. If not find out about magazine subscriptions, anything that may or may not show us what kind of man we are really dealing with. It could help narrow the field of suspects.'

Detective Constable Morris had been looking forward to getting home, however he knew there would be no rest and Mr MacLeod would work as hard, if not harder, than the rest of the team. He refrained from asking the obvious question, 'Where do I start?' He knew instinctively that no-one in the room had any idea either. He turned to his trusty computer, the only friend who could give him a clue.

'Detective Inspector Reade, leave the office work for now. You and Detective Sergeant Milton find out as much as you can about youth clubs and youth organisations. He probably isn't the rapist he is alleged to be. Maybe the married woman who was caught in the act defended herself the only way she knew how. However, as hard as it may seem to be, we should believe he is capable of this. Nothing should be overlooked.'

Detective Sergeant Milton was not too pleased that he had to work with Reade. Reade didn't know how to relax and Milton's sense of humour was not appreciated, however he shrugged his shoulders and said, 'Perhaps the caretaker Steele could give us a start.'

'I've got his address, we'll go there first,' said Reade. He was feeling a little excitement at actually getting out of the office. He was well aware that John Milton did not like him, and the feeling was mutual.

'Now, you two,' MacLeod said to Janet and Susan, 'go back to Mrs Stewart, present my compliments and tell her we need the list of 'other women'. If she argues tell her to ring the Fiscal. I will be there, he needs an update.' ('And he knows more than he is telling me too,' thought MacLeod privately. 'I can't have anyone with me when I put a little pressure on him.')

'Everyone knows what they have to do.' The team nodded in unison. 'Good, get off then and get back as soon as you can, the sooner you get back the sooner you get some rest.' 'By the way,' he said to Milton, 'Have you rung your wife and told her where you are?'

Milton replied, 'No, if I start that she will worry. She expects me when I turn up.'

142

MacLeod was stunned. He always tried to keep his wife informed of his movements, Morag would worry if he didn't. Perhaps he should have started off telling Morag that she would see him when he turned up, but it would have been unfair on her. Milton's wife was used to it after all these years. This was something he had never known about Milton in all the years he had known him. But then all marriages were different — not necessarily better, just different.

As MacLeod left the room, he saw Constable Murray who was now on sentry duty at the incident room door. The unwelcome intrusion by Helen MacDonald had upset Sergeant Gillespie very badly; he wanted no other such incursions and Murray was in no doubt that his future depended on doing his duty properly. 'Come with me, young man, I need a lift.' He was brusque. Constable Murray briefly thought he would tell Mr MacLeod that he could not leave his post, but changed his mind and meekly followed MacLeod.

'What's put a sting in his tail?' Peter Reade asked no-one in particular.

'I think the Super, he rang a few minutes ago,' said Milton.

'Strange that he hasn't mentioned about seeing Mrs Campbell again.'

'No, but he hasn't forgotten. When we saw her she was in no fit state to be interviewed properly, she should be allowed to pull herself together. We will see her tomorrow. If she gets some sleep it will do her the world of good. Whatever we get now won't be reliable.'

'I don't think she had anything to do with the murder,' said Reade, in such a pedantic tone that Milton winced, and wished that Reade would not make his mind up about things so early in an investigation. It was dangerous to assume anything. As MacLeod always said, ' 'Assume' makes an 'ass' of 'u' and 'me'.' He didn't tell Reade that MacLeod thought she was a suspect. Reade had a one-track mind and if he thought that MacLeod suspected someone he would move heaven and earth to prove it. Milton did not really approve of Reade. He was pedantic and his dotting the 'i's and crossing the 't's could get in the way of detection.

Some ten minutes later MacLeod arrived at the home of Duncan Grey. He was dropped off by Constable Murray who couldn't wait to get back to his post. Sergeant Gillespie was a fair man but did not take kindly to mistakes, even though he had to do something for a more senior officer.

MacLeod was angry that his Detective

Superintendent had told him something that Duncan Grey should have told him this morning, and was about to knock on the door when it was opened.

'Come in Cameron, I saw you coming up the drive.' They went into the living room and before he could open his mouth MacLeod was circumvented by Grey.

'I see by your face you are angry, now don't get upset, I think I know what you have found out. Yes, I know about the rumours about William and I can tell you I don't believe them. He was never a rapist. I would know that. Any proof and I would have taken him to court.'

MacLeod's eyes opened wide. 'You knew, why didn't you tell me?'

'William was dead. I didn't think, in my professional judgement, it had anything to do with his death. You obviously think so!'

'I'm surprised at you Duncan, you know that everything is important. I haven't any idea who's done this and I need every bit of help I can get, but I understand why you didn't tell me.'

'Forgiven?' Grey almost pleaded.

MacLeod paused. It was rare that a Fiscal asked a police officer for forgiveness. He relaxed and said, 'Yes, but you must tell me everything, suspicion or fact. You know

I'll keep it as quiet as possible. I don't want to give good copy to the Sunday newspapers, I hate the press, but someone may have already told them and I would have looked a complete idiot if I hadn't been privy to this.'

Duncan handed Cameron a glass containing a large malt Glenturret, eighteen years old. He sat in the armchair near the fireplace, asking MacLeod to sit opposite him.

MacLeod inhaled the gentle fumes from the glass. 'My favourite. You must be sorry. So am I, to have to come round to see you like this.'

'I think we are even. I won't ask who told you about William, but few knew about him. James Balfour did, as he was a close friend and I suspect would have known. I don't think Julia Campbell knew I only knew of it because someone told me, and I can't tell you who it was before you ask. I wanted to see if the rumours were true before I called in the police. I asked him round and put the allegation to him. He said he didn't find his wife attractive anymore and was having a deep relationship with someone else. But he did say that he didn't have to force himself on any woman. He had a problem with some who actively chased him.'

'When was this exactly?' asked MacLeod.

'Oh, about six months ago, it could have been less. I'm not sure of the date, but I could find out once I get back to the office. I did make some notes.' Grey looked at MacLeod. 'I expect you would have done so too, just in case something turned up later.'

MacLeod nodded and said, 'What on earth made him tell you this? I would have denied everything.' He sounded incredulous.

'Yes, so would I, especially when I knew I hadn't done anything wrong. If I tell you something and it gets out, someone will be investigating your murder.' Grey was serious; it wasn't said as a joke.

'Scouts' honour.' MacLeod put up his right hand showing the scout salute.

'He told me he found my wife attractive and if they had been both single he would have 'courted' her.'

MacLeod was just about to take a sip of his drink and spluttered. He looked at the photograph of Duncan's wife on the piano. She was a handsome woman, but never in a month of Sundays could she arouse anything but a maternal instinct in anyone other than her husband. 'You could say she is attractive,' MacLeod said tactfully.

'Be serious, Cameron. I love my wife but I'm not blind, she isn't a Spice Girl, more like a Girl Guide leader. I was stunned. He told me I didn't appreciate her and he thought she had a wonderful personality. I'm not a jealous person but it shook me, I became more attentive and she accused me of having an affair. I knew he was innocent of the rumours. Our friendship has cooled somewhat, but he didn't seem to notice. We have never spoken about it since.'

'What exactly were the rumours?' MacLeod wondered if Grey had more information than he had to hand.

'The usual, he was caught making love to a woman by her husband and the lady cried rape. I have no idea who it was and to be honest I didn't want to know, I would have had to do something about it if I did. There was no definite complaint, but you know how things are in a village. I had to find out, it would not be good for us if it was true and I ignored it.'

'What would you have done if he had admitted it?'

'Prosecuted him,' Grey replied without any hesitation.

MacLeod knew that Grey would never have covered up anything, friend or not. 'Did you tell anyone about it?' MacLeod asked.

'No. Oh yes! I told James Balfour, he didn't

laugh like you. He seemed genuinely shocked. I think my friend James has more sensitivity than you, you clod-hopping copper. Now, James told me that William had told him he found all women attractive but fancying someone isn't the same as doing something about it.'

'Yes, he was a handsome man, I've seen his photo. He isn't now and I wonder what happened to his head?' MacLeod was genuinely puzzled.

'I've no idea but I do hope it's found soon.' Grey shook his head, it made him sad to think about anyone being mutilated, never mind a person he knew.

'I have to get back to the office now. You will tell me if you remember anything else,' said MacLeod.

'Yes, I won't keep anything else back. It isn't fair on both of us.'

'Where does James Balfour live? I think I'll see him.'

'Only down the road, but I know he has taken his wife to her mother's in Stirling tonight. She has not stopped crying since William was found. Balfour rang to tell me, we usually see them on a Sunday night for tea. He'll be back later tonight.'

'Never mind, could you give me his telephone number at work, I'll see him tomorrow. There's one other thing you can do for me, your loyal secretary won't tell us any names, apart from one and we already know about her, unless I tell her it's vital. Perhaps you could tell her it really is essential.'

'No problem, I'll do it now.' He went to the telephone in the hallway but it rang as he touched it. Grey said with surprise, 'Maureen, I was just about to ring you.'

MacLeod noticed a group photograph on the floor of the hearth. He picked it up and a shard of glass fell out and tinkled onto the tiles. 'Careful Cameron, I just knocked it off the mantle, the glass is broken,' Grey shouted.

Looking at the photograph MacLeod noticed that the Reverend William Campbell and his wife were amongst the group, Duncan Grey and his wife, and James Balfour with a lady who Campbell presumed was his wife. Three happy innocent couples wearing climbing clothes with a backdrop of a mountain. The mountains did not appear to be Scottish Mountains. MacLeod didn't know why he thought that, it just didn't look like any mountain range he knew in Scotland.

'Where was this taken?' asked MacLeod, showing Grey the photograph as he came back into the room.

'Oh, we all went to Switzerland last year. It was the last holiday we all had together. We took a chalet and the maid took the photo for us. It's sad what a year makes. Not quite a year really, it was last October. It's a shame I dropped it. I'll have to get it re-framed.' He looked sadly at the photo. 'We looked so happy then and we were,' he sighed. 'By the way, Maureen will give your officers the list they need, in fact they are at her house now. I must tell you she would know nothing about any allegations about William, she only knows about the rumoured other women.'

'Can I ring the office to get a lift? I shouldn't have rushed out without organising a return trip.'

'Be my guest.' Grey indicated the phone without taking his gaze from the photograph. He seemed to be wishing himself back to that time when there was no slur on William's character. He remembered that day so very well. They were all happy having a wonderful time. It seemed like another life altogether.

After MacLeod had rung for his lift he came back into the room and saw Grey staring vacantly at the photograph. He had known this man for years and had never seen him so distressed. Murder was not just a violent act committed by a perpetrator on a victim; many more lives were affected deeply by the act of violence. Everyone felt guilty; that there was something they should or should not have done, if they had done this or that maybe it wouldn't have happened. Could they have averted it, could they have seen it coming?

Grey looked up, his eyes sad. MacLeod could not bring himself to say anything to try and comfort his friend; Scotsmen do not bond, and neither do they show their emotions to each other. It was not done. Instead MacLeod said, 'How's the family?' It was as close as he could get to telling Grey that he knew how he felt.

Grey cleared his throat and said, 'Fine, and yours?'

MacLeod merely said, 'Teenagers', without further comment.

'Yes, I know how you feel, all hormones and prickles. Don't worry, it will be over soon and then they will be away, off your hands. You'll miss them when it happens. The house becomes so quiet and your wife becomes another person. She's about to give you her undivided attention and it won't be any fun. No more skipping out for a quick drink. She'll start looking at what you eat and drink and she'll probably enter you for a 'fun run' to get your heart in good condition.'

'You are joking?' said MacLeod; he was horrified.

'No I'm not, I'm just going through it, the last one has flown the nest. I put my foot down at the 'fun run', though I'm getting to like the change in diet. I'm beginning to like salads.'

'Rabbit food.' MacLeod almost shouted the words. 'I'll die if I have to eat healthy food. I hate greenery,' he said, quite shocked at the future Grey had held up to his face. It was not something he relished. 'Oh dear, I've just remembered I'm going home tonight, I'd better ring Morag; she's expecting me to stay here a couple of days.'

'Go ahead, and don't forget, start your campaign for your own future now as you know what's going to happen.' Grey's mood of depression had lifted; he was enjoying the idea that MacLeod could be joining the ranks of the healthy middle-aged men in the near future. He loved it.

11

Detective Inspector Reade and Detective Sergeant Milton returned to the incident room. Reade was flustered. 'That was a waste of time. Steele's not in and no-one knows where he is.'

'I don't think it was a waste of time, Sir,' said Milton. 'I think we may have a suspect at last. I think we should circulate his description and find him. Steele had the opportunity. The motive — well that is debatable, but we will have to find him and ask him about that and I'm sure he had the means.'

'Nonsense,' said Reade, 'why would a caretaker want to kill the minister, we are not going to waste time on this.' He was in one of his most pedantic moods.

'I think we should at least try to find him, Sir. He's not at his usual haunts and no-one has seen him for hours. Don't you think we should at least try?' Milton despaired of ever seeing a true detective come out of this man's soul. 'This Detective Inspector would make a great Superintendent in Headquarters,' he thought. 'One step at a time. It's a pity

MacLeod can't see his limitations, but he is a good office manager, I'll give him that.'

In the silence that ensued Reade considered what Milton had said. He realised his irritation stemmed from Steele not being there when he wanted him, not from anything Milton had done. The world was not a tidy place at his beck and call, but it should be. He decided that Milton could have a point. 'You are probably right, Sergeant, get on with it.' He opened his mouth to say something else. 'Don't tell me he is actually going to apologise,' thought Milton. Reade changed his mind and sat down at his desk. 'Nope, I didn't think so.' Milton was sure that Reade wouldn't go that far.

Some half-hour later MacLeod returned to the incident room. As he got out of the police vehicle he thanked the Constable Murray. He was always appreciative when anyone did anything for him, remembering too well his young days when he was used as a virtual taxi service for senior officers. Of course it wouldn't happen now, for two reasons: firstly, there was far too much to do than be at the beck and call of senior officers; secondly, young officers have a sense of their own worth and such misuse of a police officer and vehicles would not be tolerated.

'I think we have a suspect: the caretaker

has done a runner and we can't find him.' Reade told MacLeod as he walked into the office.

MacLeod stopped and said, 'At last, a real suspect. He's gone has he? Well have you circulated his description?'

'Yes,' replied Reade, 'and his vehicle registration too.' Milton was delighted that Reade had taken his suggestion, but he knew he would not be granted any credit. Reade, apart from being a thorough man had another great fault: he was selfish, he liked to be at the centre of attention and it was not in his nature to allow anyone else but himself to get praise.

'Now, why would he murder the minister?' MacLeod was bemused.

'I've no idea, I never could fathom the mind of a killer,' said Milton, 'But it may not be him, he could have gone to visit relatives.'

'Nonsense,' Reade said. 'Of course it's him, he's done a runner.'

'Right, and he waited until he opened the hall for us and then decided to go; very considerate of him I'm sure.' Milton's irritation was reaching boiling point. He didn't mind Reade taking credit for his original suggestion but his attitude was grating on his nerves and he decided to give good reasons why Charlie could *not* have been the murderer to get back at this man.

Just as there seemed to be war breaking out and MacLeod was thinking he was going to have to defuse the situation, the telephone rang and Morris answered it. He turned to DCI MacLeod and said, 'Sorry Sir. Steele is out of the frame. His car has been found in Loch Eck and him in it. It looks as though he's been murdered too.'

MacLeod sighed. 'Do me a favour John,' he said to Milton. 'Every time we get a suspect for a crime something happens to them. Stop me speculating and maybe they will live longer.' Milton nodded.

Reade said, 'Perhaps we are tired and Fiery Fred pushing us to find the killer hasn't helped.'

'You are right Peter, I was happy to clear this up tonight and jumped to conclusions. Made an ass of myself again. I don't care how long this takes, we will get the right one. Come on John, let's get to the scene of the crime. We'll be back soon. Will you tell the girls they will have to go to another post-mortem, I expect the Doc will do it in the morning. Ring the Fiscal and tell him about it as well will you. I'll see him first thing in the morning. Once you've done what you have to, everyone go home and have a good night's sleep. Tiredness does not help detection.'

MacLeod and Milton left. Reade relaxed a little. Morris was looking at him with a quizzical look on his face.

'Yes, what do you want?' asked Reade.

'The boss took that well, he seemed quite excited at Steele being the murderer and now he's off to the locus of his death,' said Morris.

'My son, you will learn, the obvious suspect is rarely the perpetrator. It's a pity, it would make life easier if that were true. Whoever did this was subtle and Steele was too thick to be subtle. He would have done a runner after he committed the murder, not hung around to open up this place for us. He saw something that night, I'm sure of that, and was murdered for his knowledge. Yes, I think that's what happened.' Reade was accurate in his estimation of Charlie Steele at least. It was a pity Milton had not heard his logic. He would definitely have gone up in Milton's estimation. 'Anyway, Morris, get off home now. You need your sleep. I'll look after everything here, so off you go.'

Detective Inspector Janet MacBain and Detective Sergeant Susan Lampart arrived back at the incident room. MacLeod and

Milton walked in behind them. They had visited the locus of Charlie Steele's murder and were in sombre mood, the cold and tiredness getting into their bones. 'Shut up shop, the post-mortem is in the morning. Janet, you get there first, Susan you can go with her, eight o'clock sharp.'

Janet looked bewildered. 'Sorry, Janet, I haven't had time to tell you. The caretaker's dead and you drew the short straw again,' said MacLeod.

'I hope this one's intact,' said Susan.

'Apart from being beaten in the face with a spanner. It was considerate of the perpetrator to throw it in the car before pushing the car into the Loch. The Doc reckons he drowned, unconscious when he went in.' Milton seemed to enjoy telling her this one. 'Nothing complicated.'

'Why did he leave the weapon?' asked Susan.

'I expect he — or *she*,' MacLeod said with emphasis, 'thought the car would never be found. Loch Eck is one of the deepest lochs in Scotland but there's a small shelf, just big enough for a mini to land on. Any bigger a car and we would never have found it. Sometimes we get lucky. Now, off home with you all. See you in the morning. John, take me back to my car, my wife is expecting me, I rang her earlier. Eight o'clock sharp, apart from you two,' he pointed to the women detectives. 'You go straight to the mortuary.'

Reade said, 'I've arranged for a PC to look after the place overnight. Not out of our budget too.' He sounded satisfied. As one of the new breed of police officers he actually liked costing out the work he did. He was one of the new and one of the few. He took delight in saving money and it was his greatest pleasure to spend someone else's budget. MacLeod was also pleased but refrained from showing it. When he realised that he was delighted at actually saving on his budget he inwardly groaned. He thought that the short spell at Force headquarters had done him no good at all. Taking pleasure in saving money was not something he would have considered a few short months ago.

* * *

Ewen was sitting in the lounge of his mother's home; she had gone to bed having taken the pills that the doctor had given her. He could not sleep; he was worried about Iain. Iain was his best friend but he wasn't strong, sometimes he needed constant support, which Ewen found tiring. They had got themselves into a real pickle this time and he wasn't sure how he was going to get them out of it. His sister Shona had gone to get the last ferry.

Ewen's head was spinning. Once his mum and his sister got together he couldn't keep up with their chatter. Sometimes they changed the subject in mid sentence and he lagged behind. They knew what they were talking about but they were difficult to follow. He had given up and watched the television but he didn't remember what he had seen, his mind was elsewhere. It was peaceful now. Many of the neighbours had called in, 'to see how your Mum is,' every one of them had said as he answered the door. Rubbish! He knew they were being very nosy. 'At least Mum looked a lot better,' he thought. 'All that talking seems to have done her a lot of good.'

Ewen Jones had decided to become a lawyer. It was natural that Iain, his best friend, should follow him. Ewen had no particular ambition in life but Mr Balfour had suggested it might be a good vocation for him and having nothing else in mind, he agreed. One day he may find his true vocation, until that day he was quite happy to drift. He was a clever young man, studying was easy to him. Having a photographic memory helped. He could read a page once and it was in his head. Iain was not so fortunate; he had to work hard and relied upon Ewen to help him.

Ewen half closed the curtains; it was getting very late but it was still light enough to see the kirk from the window. He gained a fleeting impression from the buildings of extreme sadness. He wondered at this. He had always thought of the kirk as a happy place. The events of the last 24 hours had put a dampener on everything, including his normal high spirits. If only the clock could be put back. One of their neighbours had come in to tell a hushed audience that there had been a second murder: Charlie Steele had been found in his car in Loch Eck.

Somehow this news seemed to cheer up his mum. It was as if it cleared something in her mind. It diminished the death of the Reverend Campbell somehow. But *two* murders in one day, here in Kilmun. It didn't bear thinking about. Usually people didn't lock their doors at night, but tonight they did.

Ewen saw the last streaks of sunlight disappear and sparkling dots of light appeared in the sky. When he was in Glasgow he had to look straight up to see any stars. The lights of the city overshadowed the night sky. At home he could see stars almost to

162

the horizon. The naval base at Coulport was lit up like a town and caused an eerie glow blocking out the stars on the horizon if he looked in that direction. Mostly he avoided looking at the place. It was definitely a blot on the landscape by day and night. He wondered how much their light bill was; his mum always complained about their electricity bill. Perhaps there was someone like his mum at Coulport, who would switch off unnecessary lights. Or perhaps not; he was just old enough to know that government departments were not too careful with money, after all it wasn't theirs.

Ewen went to the bottom of the stairs and listened for his mother. There was no noise from the bedroom. 'Fast asleep, and I hope she stays that way, it will do her good, and I can do what I have to do without being disturbed!' He shuddered. Going to the cupboard under the stairs where the electricity meter was, he put the light on and picked up his haversack. A darkening reddish brown stain covered the bottom. He swore under his breath. There was a reddish brown stain on the floorboards too. He went into the kitchen and got a black bin liner. He put the haversack in the bin liner and went out.

He knew the contents of the haversack but

did not have the courage to open it just then. He gingerly carried the bag and crept towards the kirk. He heard a noise and stopped. In the dark he saw the glow of a cigarette, and smelt the smoke drifting towards him. Just then the moon appeared from behind a cloud and the silvery light illuminated a police officer leaning on the wall of the kirk looking towards him. Ewen stopped in his tracks and his heart missed a beat, but to his relief a voice in the distance shouted, 'Tea up.' The constable turned round and left his post. He obviously hadn't seen Ewen, and for that Ewen gave a thankful prayer.

Ewen went into the old ruin. After taking the haversack out of the bin liner he pushed it onto a ledge at the left side of the entrance. In the darkness it would not be seen and in the light he hoped it would be missed in the recess. He knew the ruin had been searched, he had seen it done from his bedroom, by at least two young policemen. Ewen didn't recognise them but laughed when one of them fell headlong into the doorless entrance.

Ewen opened the haversack and gingerly removed its contents. He gagged as he looked at the head of the Reverend Campbell. It looked like a waxwork. All the blood had drained from its features, giving a blue-grey hue that shone in the moonlight. Once he had hidden the head hopefully no-one would find it for some time, in fact he was hoping no-one ever would.

When he got back home he put some bleach and water into a bucket and scrubbed the wooden floor under the stairs, but it didn't seem to do any good. He wondered whether he should ask his mum how to get blood out of wood, but changed his mind. That really would have made her wonder. He put an old carpet over the stains and hoped she wouldn't go into the cupboard under the stairs too soon. He could smell the bleach mixed with dirt and blood. It would fade soon, he hoped, but just now it was overpowering.

Ewen went to bed and had a fitful night's sleep. He had nightmares about heads and policemen and cells. He woke a couple of times in a cold sweat and wished he had his mother's pills. He wondered whether he would ever sleep well again.

12

Detective Inspector Janet MacBain and Detective Sergeant Susan Lampart walked out of the mortuary into clean, fresh air and gulped for breath. Twice in a matter of days they had attended a post-mortem. 'I don't know how anyone can work there all the time,' said Susan.

'Maybe they get used to it and don't notice the smells. I know that I couldn't do it,' replied Janet.

They had been to the post-mortem of Charles Steele. It was confirmed by Doctor Ellis that he had indeed drowned after being rendered unconscious with a heavy spanner. The marks on the face and underlying skull fitted the damage done by a heavy blow. If he hadn't drowned it was unlikely he would have survived the blow. His teeth, cheekbones, forehead and nasal cavities had sustained such injuries that drowning was a more merciful death. His lungs contained a mixture of blood and water.

'Before we get onto the next job I need a cup of coffee,' said Janet. 'Only coffee?' said Susan. Janet used her mobile phone to ring the incident room and reported the results of the post-mortem to Detective Inspector Peter Reade. Susan overheard her say, 'No, it wasn't a suicide, if it was he pushed his own car into the Loch after he fell unconscious.' Janet tried to keep the irritation out of her voice. After she had disconnected the call she took a deep breath. 'What did we do before mobile phones?' she asked. 'Ran backwards and forwards like lunatics — we really needed the shoe allowance then. Most of our radios didn't work around here; there was no other choice.'

It was relatively quiet in Black the Bakers. They sat in the small tea-room, which was nicely decorated and comfortable, tucked to the left off the main bakery counter. Scotch pies were being baked in the back of the shop. The smell of these award-winning pies was too much for Janet, and she succumbed to temptation. She had also given in to a piece of pecan and maple pastry, which had melted in her mouth.

'I'm shocked at you,' said Susan.

'What do you mean?' Janet looked at her with surprise. 'Your diet has gone to hell, you've had enough and I think you are about to get another cake.'

'How do you know that?' asked Janet.

'I've known you long enough to know that

look in your eyes.' Susan put her head to one side and gave Janet a stern look.

'I can't help it, when I go on a diet I become hungry.' Janet was contrite. 'We'll get out of here before I go really berserk and have a fresh cream cake with fresh cream and fruit. Heaven help me. This place should have a diet warning.'

'You should go on my father's diet. He says it works — eat anything you want and every six months buy bigger clothes!' Susan was joking of course. She wanted to help Janet diet if she really wanted to lose weight, but she refused to waste her energy on a lost cause. At least she didn't have a meringue. Fiery Fred would have been proud of her.

They walked out into the brilliant sunshine. A lot of money had been spent on refurbishing the town centre. Footpaths had been widened and barriers made of wrought iron with a Gaelic touch had been erected. The changes made to Argyll Street, the sunshine and the half-clad holidaymakers gave an almost Mediterranean feel to the place.

In the car Susan brought out the list of women the Reverend Campbell was supposed to have had affairs with. 'Do you believe this? I don't,' said Susan.

'What do you mean?' asked Janet, genuinely puzzled.

'Well, a man of the cloth having affairs like this. Perhaps he was a 'loveaholic', the same as you are a foodaholic.' Susan smiled. She enjoyed giving her friend a dig now and again and hoped that the reason behind her present binge could be brought out. Susan dearly wanted to help, but felt frustrated at Janet's refusal to talk.

'I'm not addicted to food, it's just that I can't resist it.' Janet was indignant. Susan burst out laughing, and held her sides. It was the first time she had laughed out loud since her lover, Jo, had been taken into hospital. As she laughed that thought entered her head and she stopped abruptly. She felt guilty that she could laugh when everything at home was so serious.

Janet understood why she had stopped laughing and gently said, 'Don't feel guilty about laughing. Jo wouldn't like you to be miserable, you know that.' Susan nodded, but there were tears in her eyes, a mixture of happiness and pain.

'Right! Lets get on to business. Who's the first one to see?' Janet was abruptly efficient bringing Susan's mind back to the job in hand and taking her own mind off her problems too.

At the other end of town Mr James Balfour sat in his office in Hillfoot Street. It was high on the hill overlooking the Clyde, giving a magnificent view of the hills of Renfrewshire and North Ayrshire. Normally he viewed his domain with some satisfaction but not today. Today he was still shaken by the events of the weekend. The intercom bleeped, his secretary Jean announced that Detective Chief Inspector MacLeod and Detective Sergeant Milton were in the outer office wishing to see him.

'They tell me they have an appointment, but I don't see it in the book.' Jean sounded petulant. She was the organiser of his office and took umbrage when he forgot to tell her something she felt she should know.

'Sorry Jean, I should have told you, they rang before you got in. Give me a couple of minutes.' He went to the small anteroom and splashed water on his face. Looking in the mirror he saw his haggard features. It came as a shock, the change over a mere 24 hours. He could hardly look at his own face whilst he combed his hair and tidied himself up.

Pushing the intercom button he said, 'Please send my guests in Jean.' Balfour was always polite to his staff; he felt obliged to them for running his office whilst he was out, even though he paid them for doing it.

As MacLeod walked into the office he was delighted to see an old-fashioned lawyer's office, none of the newfangled shine and gleam of chrome beloved of the modern lawyer. There was no computer, just an inkwell and even a quill. MacLeod sensed that Balfour was a man who followed tradition. The inkwell was obviously in use: there was a well-worn and used fountain pen lying beside the blotting pad, and smudges of ink from writing were evident. He didn't even use cartridges but the quill was strictly for decoration only.

The side walls of the office were lined with shelves upon which great leather bound tomes were kept clean and dusted. The wall facing the desk was covered with framed documents and personal photographs. MacLeod glanced at this wall with interest and saw the same photograph he had seen in the Fiscal's home. It must really have been a happy holiday for this photograph to be framed by two of the couples pictured. He wondered if the Campbells had a similar framed photograph.

The only concession Balfour seemed to have given to any form of modernisation of the office was the picture frame double-glazed window behind his large leather chair, which gave a panoramic view of the Clyde estuary and the hills of Ayrshire beyond. Balfour indicated the two leather chairs in front of his desk, shiny with years of use and surprisingly comfortable, as the two detectives discovered when they sat down.

When they were seated, Balfour asked if they would like coffee. The offer of a caffeine boost was gratefully accepted. MacLeod looked at Balfour and noted how his appearance had deteriorated from the day before. The hollow-eyed man who appeared before him now was a stranger to the man he had seen yesterday. Balfour was on edge and appeared to have been crying.

'How long have you known the Reverend Campbell?' asked MacLeod.

'Nearly all my life. You see we grew up together in the same area of Glasgow. We went to school together, in fact you could say we were best friends then. When we went to University we drifted apart. William was clever, he managed to get a scholarship and went to Divinity School. I was as good as he was, but my family couldn't support me through University, so I managed to get an Army Scholarship.'

'An Army Scholarship! You were in

the Army!' Milton somehow couldn't see Balfour in the Army. Granted he was tall and reasonably fit, but he didn't have the bearing of an ex-army officer, that indefinable something that the Army marks on their volunteers for life.

'I didn't do a long stint, they paid my way through University and all you had to give back in those days was three years. It may be different now. It wasn't too hard. I was with the Army Legal Service in the Far East. In fact I enjoyed it and I know I grew up there.' Balfour smiled at his memories, but did not elaborate for his audience; he remembered a particular nurse who was a great deal older than him with both pleasure and gratitude. The haggard look on his face receded a little and he became more of the man he was a mere eight hours earlier. He was still thinking about his first love when MacLeod's voice thundered into his consciousness.

'Could you tell me about Mr Campbell? I really need to know everything, we need all the help we can get.' MacLeod leaned forward and touched his arm.

Balfour shook himself and said, 'Sorry, I was miles away. I was going to tell you I didn't really know him but I've decided to tell you the truth. He was very attractive you know. Even when he was young, the women

173

fell over themselves to be with him.'

'Did he, how shall I put it, ever force his attentions on a woman?' MacLeod decided to be direct.

'Never, he didn't need to. I know the rumours about him, but I assure you he had all the charm of the devil.' Balfour suddenly realised what he had said and hastily added, 'I didn't mean he was evil or anything, in fact he was the opposite. Oh Dear! I think I may have given you the wrong impression,'

MacLeod said, 'I don't think so, I understand what you mean. You know about the rumours. You know — forcing himself on a woman. Do you know who it was?'

Balfour said without hesitation, 'No, I do not know who it was, if I find out I will do my duty and tell you.'

'Could you tell me where you were on Saturday evening?' MacLeod decided to be direct.

'Ah! I'm a suspect too am I? Well, it's natural I suppose. You will have to ask everyone he knew, but I didn't have a motive you know,' Balfour remarked without any sign of offence. 'I was at home with my wife. She is with her mother in Stirling at the moment. She was devastated at the news, she's very sensitive you know, and not very well — women's troubles. I'll be glad when the menopause is over.'

MacLeod stiffened. He hated any mention of 'women's problems'. He had enough with teenage girl problems. He asked Balfour, 'Could we see her? She seems to have been a close friend of the family too. Perhaps she will be able to say more?'

'I'm afraid not. Once she is better I will bring her to you. I am not being over-protective I assure you, but I would rather you didn't disturb her at the moment if you don't mind,' Balfour replied.

MacLeod did mind and made a mental note to find out where Mrs Balfour's mother lived, with or without her husband's co-operation, and make a visit as soon as possible. He felt she had information that could help him, but he said, 'Not at all, there's no rush.'

MacLeod cleared his throat and said, 'I must ask you if you knew of any of the affairs William Campbell had. I assure you we will be discreet.'

'I only know he was a butterfly. But he only had one grand passion at a time. He preferred older women; maturity attracted him more than youth. He preferred the company of people his own age, like me, he found experience a greater turn on than frivolous youth.' Balfour stopped, he realised he may have given the wrong impression. MacLeod was no fool.

'Are you saying you and he are the same?' MacLeod had indeed picked up on the nuance of the last remark.

'No, I'm not saying that. I am faithful to my wife but I do prefer the company of people my own age.' Balfour was emphatic. 'And in reply to your question about any liaisons he had I only know of Mrs Jones, the receptionist at the Health Centre. She made no secret of it. She was a little indiscreet at times. Julia knew and both my wife and I knew. Julia was terribly jealous but William found jealousy a strange emotion, you see, he never suffered from it. In some respects he was a cold fish.'

'Can you tell me how he got on with his wife?' asked MacLeod. 'That's the strange thing, he didn't treat her as his wife, it was funny. They were more like brother and sister, they bickered a lot, which could be embarrassing in public, but there didn't seem to be any marital love there. I think he was fond of her really.' Balfour stopped and thought for a moment. 'Sometimes Julia can be a strange person, one minute she was jovial and the next she seemed to become someone else. It didn't happen often and she always apologised. She said it was due to her illness, she's not a well woman. She didn't show her feelings except where Mrs Jones was concerned. My wife told me that Julia was very jealous but I didn't see it.'

'Now could you tell me where you were on Sunday afternoon?' MacLeod changed the subject quickly; it was a good ploy that kept the subject from being comfortable.

Balfour was certainly uncomfortable. 'What? I don't know.'

'It was only yesterday, Mr Balfour,' MacLeod said.

'Oh, I took my wife to Stirling.'

'What time was that?' asked MacLeod.

'I don't know, after lunch.' Balfour sounded vague.

MacLeod turned to Milton and said, 'Give me your notes.' As Milton handed the notes over to MacLeod he asked Balfour, 'Would you go past Loch Eck to get to Stirling?'

Turning to Milton, Balfour replied, 'No, we took the Ferry, we didn't go by Loch Eck. Why are you asking?'

MacLeod said as he looked up from the notes he'd been studying, 'Mr Charlie Steele was found murdered on the Loch Eck road on Sunday evening.'

'Oh my! I knew him well. I suppose I'm a

suspect for that too?' Balfour was becoming irritated.

'Not at all, but we have to ask.' MacLeod was pleasant in his manner, which seemed to irritate Balfour more.

'I'm sorry.' Balfour seemed to inwardly collapse. 'Its all too much, I think I should go home and get some rest. I haven't slept all night.'

MacLeod closed the notebook and stared at Balfour intently. He had many more questions to put to him but decided to see Balfour's wife first to be on surer ground. Balfour's face had gone white and he looked as if he were about to throw up. MacLeod decided to see this man at a later date and said, 'Yes, I think you should, you really don't look well. Maybe you should consider seeing a doctor.'

Balfour gave him a weak smile. 'Jean, my secretary has already nagged me about that, but I don't like doctors, and I hate needles.'

MacLeod asked almost as an afterthought, 'How did you both happen to live here? It's a strange coincidence isn't it?'

'Not so strange, I left the Army and joined a practice in Glasgow. My wife's father was a lawyer with a practice in Dunoon, through work I met him and he introduced me to his daughter who became my wife. It was natural that I should join him here, keeping it in the family so to speak. When he retired to Stirling I took over his practice. William turned up about fifteen years ago.' Balfour paused and remembered his delight at seeing his old friend again. His eyes relaxed for a moment. 'We had been in contact, you know, Christmas cards, birthdays that sort of thing. It was lovely to see him again and we took up our friendship where we had left off. Fran, my wife and Julia became good friends. Our children grew up together. In fact they only separated when my two went to University in England. Iain decided to go to a Scottish University.' Balfour paused and seemed to be struggling for words; he then made a decision to describe William as honestly as he could. 'Mr MacLeod, you must understand. William was everything I would have liked to be. He was popular, made friends easily and was a very good minister. The only flaw he had was that he was amoral. He wasn't immoral; he didn't really know the meaning of the word 'moral', even though he preached against immorality. So long as no-one got hurt, he gaily went about life doing his own thing. He thought he was spreading happiness. He was like that, even as a child. He gave so much, he was full of life and loving. It was impossible not to like him.'

MacLeod said, 'I understand, I've met the type myself.' Although he did not add his total disapproval of the havoc caused to those around such people.'

'I think that is all I can tell you. Is there anything else?'

MacLeod replied, 'No, but if you think of anything else please, don't hesitate in contacting me.'

★ ★ ★

Later whilst they were travelling back to the incident room Milton said, 'I think Mr Balfour was jealous of his friend.'

MacLeod agreed and said, 'There's a lot Mr James Balfour hasn't told us. Do you get the impression that we are being told only so much and nothing more by everyone in this case? There are no lies, only half truths, which are worse than outright lies.'

Milton said, 'Did you get a good look at the photograph of the couples? Campbell is looking at Mrs Balfour, Balfour is looking at Campbell. Maybe I'm wrong, but I think Mrs Balfour had a fling with Campbell and I think our fine lawyer knew it.'

'Yes, I noticed it and did you notice that

the one question everyone asks he omitted to do so?'

'What's that?' Milton was curious.

'When I told him Charlie Steele had been murdered he didn't ask how it had happened.'

'Yes, I noticed but he was so wound up over something it could have been an oversight,' said Milton.

'Perhaps, anyway I think your theory of a fling with his wife wasn't a strong motive, Campbell was moving on.'

'Did you also get the impression that he was going to say something different when he said he had a confession to make?' asked Milton.

'Yes, he changed his mind.' MacLeod stopped speaking for a moment then said, 'Pull over.'

'What's the matter?' asked Milton when he had parked the car in the nearest lay-by.

'Do you think the Fiscal had anything to do with Campbell moving from here? asked MacLeod. 'You know, just like the police force, if there is a problem move it on.'

'I would say so, but don't blame him, you've done it a few times in your career.'

MacLeod smiled sure that his friend Grey was devious and underhand as only he could be. He recognised some of his own qualities in Grey's actions. He had some suspicions that Grey could have been the murderer of Campbell, but now it settled in his mind Grey was moving his problem on. There would be no need to kill him. He would check out Grey's movements just in case. It would have to be done discreetly or he could find himself transferred. He may not be a problem at the moment to the Fiscal, but if he upset him and his suspicions were wrong! The Fiscal's power was absolute, and MacLeod liked working in this area. Balfour had no reason to murder Campbell. If his wife were having an affair with Campbell the posting would solve his problem too. A word in the right ear within the hierarchy of the kirk and Campbell would be moved, of that MacLeod was sure.

MacLeod wondered whether he could 'persuade' the higher authorities to reveal the reasons why Campbell was moving on. He remembered, as a young detective, investigating a minister of the Cloth for indecency with children. This man had been moved twice before, he had been singularly unsuccessful in getting anyone in authority to admit that he had done anything of a similar nature before, even when he had produced proof of the criminal activities.

No, approaching the authorities would

be frustrating and fruitless. He would concentrate on other paths. He had no intention of being diverted down a blind alley. Even if Campbell had been moved for 'infidelities' it may not bring him closer to the killer. The information lay somewhere, he and his team would find it.

13

Detective Superintendent Thomson was sitting in the incident room. He had been given a cup of coffee. He was amused by the antics of the young officer who had been sitting at the computer screen. First he had fidgeted, then he seemed to get so uncomfortable he had got up and sidled out of the room.

'I think you make our young officer nervous Sir,' said Detective Inspector Peter Reade.

'I wonder why?' said Thomson. 'I'm not that much of an ogre, am I?'

Reade was debating with himself whether or not to tell the truth, that in his opinion Thomson was a bully and perfectionist with a tendency to browbeat anyone who disagreed with him. He was also wondering what effect such candour would have on his career when Detective Chief Inspector Cameron MacLeod accompanied by Detective Sergeant John Milton came into the room. He took the excuse of their arrival to ignore the question posed.

'Hello Sir, what brings you over here?' said MacLeod.

'Too many questions at Force Headquarters.

There's a second body and I can't even speculate on the reasons why the first happened. We don't have anyone in the frame do we?'

MacLeod replied, 'No, but it's early days yet.'

Thomson got up from the chair and went to the incident board. 'Is this the second body?'

'Yes, one Charlie Steele, the caretaker for the kirk,' said MacLeod. 'It's unfortunate because he became the prime suspect. He obviously saw something and decided to contact the killer instead of us.'

'Do you think these two murders are connected?' asked Thomson.

'Aye, I'm sure. The last murder in Kilmun is so far back no-one can remember when. Two murders, especially two people who knew each other, are particularly suspicious.'

'I suppose so, a greedy man this Steele. Made the same mistake of all blackmailers. I can never understand anyone trying to blackmail a murderer. If he or she killed once there's nothing to stop them killing again.'

'If he'd had any sense he would have told us what he saw then sold his story to the newspapers. He probably would have got more for it too,' said Milton.

'No, he couldn't do that — well, he could but he would have to wait a long time before being paid. After the trial would be the earliest. You met Steele, did he give you the impression of being a patient man?' asked MacLeod.

Milton thought for a few seconds, 'No, you are right. I only met him for a few minutes, but he came over as a man who lived for today.'

MacLeod turned to Thomson, 'Could I have a word with you in private, please?' In the small office Thomson said, 'It must be serious, you rarely keep anything from your team.'

'Yes and no. Could you do me a favour and see the Fiscal? Now I don't think he had anything to do with the murders but he seems to be closely involved with all this and I really need to know where he was when both murders were perpetrated.'

Thomson's eye's widened. 'I'll do what you ask but if he takes the hump and I get posted back into uniform you'll be coming with me, understand?'

MacLeod nodded, upset at having to ask his boss to do this for him, but the Fiscal's dignity and his friendship were involved. He knew his friend was innocent but the questions had to be asked.

There was a sudden commotion in the outer office. Thomson and MacLeod hurried out to see what it was all about. Milton was holding Detective Constable Morris by the shoulders. Morris's eyes were wide, he was gasping for breath, his face was white and his hair dishevelled.

'What's the matter son?' Milton said as he shook Morris by the shoulders.

Morris was almost incoherent but he eventually managed to say, 'I've found the head. It's in the old tower.'

MacLeod was startled. 'I thought the whole area was searched. Reade, check with Sergeant Gillespie, find out who searched the tower and whether they missed it.' Reade nodded and went to his desk to ring the local police station.

Thomson turned to Morris. 'Take me to the locus son.' He was gentle, for which MacLeod and Milton were extremely grateful. Young Morris was not hardened yet to either police work or the overbearing tactics of some senior officers.

Thomson and MacLeod accompanied Morris to the tower at the west side of the kirk; MacLeod had Morris by the arm and was propelling him back to the scene. Morris had no desire to go back but realised he could not fight against MacLeod's restraining hold. MacLeod was too strong for him, though all his senses told him not to go back and he wanted to run away, screaming his fear; he was using all his willpower not to do so.

'It's over there.' Morris pointed to the iron gated entrance of the tower.

The modern mesh railing had been partially removed earlier to allow entry by the police search team. MacLeod went to the doorway and peering in he saw, in a small niche at the left hand side of the closed gate, the head of the Reverend William Campbell. It was lying on it's back. The eyes were open. The tongue was enlarged and filled the mouth, it was blue black and dried blood streaked down the centre where in life the teeth had clamped down tight.

'Get back to the incident room and get someone to tape off the tower, then get a uniformed constable at the entrance to stop anyone going in.' MacLeod released his grip on Morris's arm and gave him a gentle push to get him going. Morris was almost catatonic now and needed something to do until his inner panic had subsided. It wasn't a pretty sight for anyone, least of all a sensitive soul like Morris.

Detective Inspector Janet MacBain and Detective Sergeant Susan Lampart had returned to the incident room whilst MacLeod and Thomson were still at the tower. Reade had contacted Sergeant Gillespie who confirmed that he had supervised the search of the tower and there was no head there, he was positive.

'Why on earth did you decide to search the tower again?' Susan asked Morris.

'It was the Detective Superintendent, he made me so nervous I had to get out and I just wandered about. I found myself there. I'm interested in the history of the tower and when I looked through the gate I noticed a lump. The gate was locked so I found a stick and poked at it. The head rolled out.' He shuddered. 'It was awful.'

No-one in the room laughed then, but much later they all saw the funny side of it. For the rest of his service Morris suffered from mannequin's heads appearing in his desk drawer or on his computer or chair with regular monotony, much to his annoyance.

Thomson and MacLeod came into the room. MacLeod said, 'It's time for a conference, this case is getting more and more bizarre.'

Reade told Thomson and MacLeod that Sergeant Gillespie had searched the tower himself.

'Well if he did, then I know it was done properly, someone must have put the head there last night. Have you contacted the pathologist?'

Reade confirmed that Doctor Ellis, the pathologist, was on his way, also a forensic team and the photographer.

Just as the team had settled down with their notes to brief both Thomson and MacLeod, Doctor Ellis appeared in the doorway, 'Got it then, good work, I'll get onto it once the photographer has finished.'

'Just a moment Doc, can I have a word?' MacLeod went to the door and took the doctor outside. 'Did you thoroughly examine Campbell's body?'

Ellis was startled and a little affronted. 'Of course I did,' he said. 'Here's my report.' He handed MacLeod a folder. 'I'll send my bill later, but if you don't explain your insulting question I'll double it.'

'There's been an allegation that he was a rapist and it's turning my stomach. I know you can't tell if he is one but I was hoping there may be something, anything to indicate he was a deviant or otherwise.' MacLeod sounded hopeful.

Doctor Ellis was stunned, 'I did thoroughly check. His rectum and anal area were perfectly normal, apart from a slight case of haemorrhoids. I did check everywhere and I can tell you he had recently had sexual intercourse. It's all in the report.' He calmed down from his initial prickly reaction. 'I can't tell you what you want to know but I haven't got the results of the blood tests as yet; there may be something there, though I doubt it. I hate rapists as much as you do but forensically they are no different to you or I.'

MacLeod smiled. He really must keep that one in mind when he had to attend his children's school, to have a doctor say that a rapist is outwardly as normal as any man would perhaps bring home to children the dangers of going with strange men. Some of the teachers would be horrified but perhaps he could get the message through. Then he thought of Morag's reaction and changed his mind. His wife would be so embarrassed and Jacqueline too, though perhaps Nicola would enjoy his forthright comments. Yes Jacqueline was much the quieter one. Nicola would take on the world and spit out the bones.

MacLeod returned to the incident room. Thomson looked at him with questions in his eyes. MacLeod shook his head and said, 'Later.'

'Right, let's get on with it.' MacLeod

turned to the team. 'Detective Inspector MacBain, what are your results?'

'We were sent to see the five women who allegedly had affairs with the Reverend Campbell. All five did have relationships with him varying from close friendship to full blown affairs. We had to see two of them well away from their homes. In one case it was because her new husband was about to come in from the garden. The second didn't want her family to know. All the women had nothing but praise and warm affection for Campbell and have remained friends with him. The relationships varied from a few weeks to a few months, nothing lasted longer than two years, and from the dates they gave us, none of them were overlapping,' said Janet.

'In your opinion were any of them capable of killing him?'

Both Janet and Susan thought for a while. MacLeod was patient, he preferred a considered answer rather than a hot headed one. 'No, I don't think so,' said Janet.

'What about you Detective Sergeant Lampart?'

Susan answered immediately as she had had time to think. 'No, definitely not. I don't believe they could. They liked him too much.'

'What about their families?' asked MacLeod. 'Well, that's debatable, we would have to interview the families but to do that we would have to break the trust that these ladies have put in us as they assure us that their families don't know. I think we could quietly check them out, but not up front. No,' she shook her head, 'it wouldn't be a good idea to see the families, it may cause a great deal of unnecessary upset and harm.'

'If you found out about them, why should their families be different and not know?' demanded Thomson.

'It's like this Sir,' said Janet, 'What women know and will talk about to each other is not generally spoken about to men or children.'

'I agree,' said Susan. 'This is a place where women will talk to other women but not necessarily to their menfolk.' They looked at each other.

MacLeod completely understood. Sometimes at home he felt an outsider when he walked in on his wife and two girls, it was as if he was intruding into another world. Thomson had a similar feeling in his own home, and it irritated him. It was as if there was an area in life he could never be a part of. Unlike MacLeod who could be sensitive and accept the situation. Thomson really could not accept an area in his sphere of influence he could neither be a part of nor control. 'All right, I accept your assessments, but if we have no alternative we will have to question the families at a later stage. Now let's get a real idea of where we are and what needs to be done. Detective Inspector Reade, a briefing if you please.'

Peter Reade stood up and went to the blackboard where there was a map drawn of the house and kirk. He picked up an old fashioned pointer — no laser light pointer for him. 'Campbell was last seen by his wife at six o'clock on Saturday evening. We haven't got anyone else who saw him later than that. If he walked from here,' indicating a house on the map, 'along this road,' he pointed carefully along the front, 'to the kirk here, it would have taken him about twenty minutes. Mrs Jones said she heard someone at nine o'clock or so, it may have been the Reverend Campbell, if so, there's some three hours missing between his leaving home and the site of his death.'

'Perhaps he spent all the time in the kirk,' said Milton.

'Perhaps he had company,' Janet added and smiled.

'I don't think so,' said Thomson. 'The kirk was always open and if he was meeting a woman . . . '

'Or man. He may not have had a sexual assignation at all,' interrupted MacLeod. 'All right, man or woman, but if he were meeting a woman he wouldn't take a chance in an open place. It would be at their home within walking distance of his home. He didn't take his car and he wasn't seen by anyone; or perhaps he was picked up by the lady?' said Thomson.

'I don't think he was 'picked up' as you put it, Sir. Nothing unusual was seen and the local Reverend getting into or out of a lady's car would definitely have been reported,' said Reade.

MacLeod's brain was ticking over. 'Not necessarily, it was a wild night and few people were around . . . but have we had the kirk grounds thoroughly checked?' he asked.

Reade replied, 'Not really and there is a small building at the side of the cemetery. It's used as a storeroom now but it was used in the last century as a guardhouse for the graves. The graveyard was guarded to prevent grave-robbers. I do know it's got a camp bed in it. Perhaps they met there, the footpaths to and from the hut can't be seen from the road. Maybe we'll be lucky.'

'While you are at it, get this whole area searched again, and get the night shift boys interviewed. They may have seen something, though it's doubtful. They missed the head being deposited in the tower. If they did see anything and didn't report it then I want to see them,' said MacLeod.

Milton looked at Reade. Both had been on the wrong end of MacLeod's tongue and remembered it without pleasure.

'Cheeky doing that,' said Susan, 'waiting until the tower was searched then putting the head there. Whoever did it thought it wouldn't be found for a long time.'

'Right, a list of suspects is needed. Just a list, we'll think about it later and narrow the field. I'll put forward Mrs Jones: jealousy because he dumped her,' said MacLeod.

'How about her son Ewen and his pal Iain, the Reverend's son? They could have found out about the Reverend's infidelity,' said Susan.

'Either alone or together,' added Janet.

MacLeod nodded. 'Get their movements properly checked out. Convenient they were inside a cell for part of the night. Next . . . ' He looked at Reade.

'When we find out who he was having his latest affair with, either her or her husband.' Reade couldn't think of anything else to say.

'It's a pretty short list,' said Thomson.

'Why are we concentrating on jealousy as a motive?'

'The murder was done in such a manner that it tells us that Campbell was a traitor, the same as his forefather. A pretty crude way of showing us, but nonetheless it was done that way and everything we have found out about our irreverent gentleman shows he was a ladies' man. Jealousy is a pretty powerful motive,' said MacLeod.

'Maybe it was a smoke screen,' said Thomson. 'Yes, but somehow I don't think so. Until we eliminate everyone who could have been jealous from the list I don't propose to extend it,' said MacLeod.

'Oh, Boss, I forgot to tell you, I've traced the knife through the Imperial War Museum,' Morris piped up. 'It's an Australian bayonet, it was an experiment in the 1940s to combine a bayonet with a machete. There were quite a few made but not millions like other bayonets.'

MacLeod's eyes widened. 'So, we have to find someone who has military connections as well.'

'Round here!' exclaimed Milton. 'Every other family has military connections. It's one of the biggest reasons for children leaving home, no job or the Army. What would you choose?'

'Have we forgotten Mrs Campbell in all this,' said Janet quietly. 'She had one of the best reasons to kill him and I think she had the strength to do so, or she got her son to help her. She's been humiliated all these years and probably cracked at last.'

Thomson heard her and said, 'His wife? The minister's wife? Never! She had been wronged for years. Why now? They were moving on to pastures new, perhaps starting a new life. Do you really think so?'

'Yes,' Janet replied. 'Maybe 'the pastures new' was a new female population to plunder.'

Thomson said, 'Fine, put her on the list, but I'll put money on it; she has nothing to do with this.'

MacLeod half heard the exchange. His mind was on other things: he was thinking. 'Was Campbell a rapist?' He strongly doubted it. 'But where had the allegation come from?'

When the conference dispersed he said to Thomson, 'Could you please find out from your mother exactly where the information came from about Campbell's alleged attack on a woman? I think it will be useful.'

14

After the conference MacLeod sat in his office flicking through the notes made of the information he had to date. He thought back to his interview with James Balfour, lawyer of this parish, elder of the church and close friend of the victim. A respected member of the community who said he didn't know in detail of any affairs that Campbell had embarked upon during their friendship. Surely such close friends would know; he had known him since boyhood after all.

MacLeod felt he was being severely misled by someone who had spread the slur about Campbell having raped a woman. This was a totally premeditated and planned murder. MacLeod realised that there had been a deliberate and possibly unfounded accusation made against Campbell for a reason he had yet to fathom.

The murder of Charlie Steele was different. That had the feel of a panic murder. The car had been pushed into the Loch, but by chance it was at the shallowest part. If it had been pushed a couple of hundred yards further down the road and it would never have been found. No, the Reverend William Campbell's murder had not been on impulse; he felt that in his bones; but committed by whom? Perhaps Janet was right; his wife had finally cracked and done it. He may have only half-heard Janet but he had noted what she had said. She had impeccable logic.

Balfour had been in the Army in the Far East; could he have picked up the strange Australian machete bayonet then? Was he Mrs Campbell's accomplice? Why did Balfour take his wife to Stirling? What about the boys? What about Mrs Jones? Where did the Fiscal fit in? Too many questions and not enough answers.

Thomson came back from the Fiscal's house in a good mood. Turning to MacLeod he said, 'I've done your dirty work for you. Duncan Grey can be cleared of any involvement. I asked him outright where he was when both murders were committed and when he stopped laughing, he told me that you should have asked him yourself. He wasn't offended at all and we aren't getting posted. He was with his wife on the Saturday, I believe him, and on the Sunday he was having lunch with his neighbours the Webbs. He also said that he remembered who told him that Campbell had been caught in the act of rape, it was one of the elders.'

'Don't tell me, Mr James Balfour.'

'So the Fiscal lied to me, he told me that he had told James Balfour of the allegations of rape, not the other way round.'

MacLeod thought, 'Or maybe he is protecting his source of information and lying to Thomson. Whatever, it doesn't matter now, the main thing is that Duncan Grey had been asked. It would be for a later date to re-question Grey.' MacLeod filed his doubts for future reference.

'Yes, how did you know?' Thomson was surprised:

'I didn't, a lucky guess.' MacLeod was gloomy. He liked Balfour. In his job he found it difficult to like any lawyer, but this man was different. He somehow felt sorry for him; if he was a murderer it would haunt him for the rest of his life. He would never be able to come to terms with his action. Planning something is not the same as carrying it out. Most murderers forget the effect the worst of crimes can have on themselves. Killing is not easy at all and murderers always destroy themselves as well as their victims. Sympathy for Balfour could be an emotion that could interfere with the investigation as he always said and he shook himself out of his present mood. Turning to Thomson he said, 'Are you staying on, Sir?'

'No, unfortunately not, I've been ordered back to Force HQ. I hate these things.' He shook his mobile phone, 'I knew I shouldn't have answered it. Sometimes they are more interference than assistance. I've to report to the Assistant Chief Constable on the progress of the investigation; he's taking a personal interest. You know Mackenzie, a real Christian, he goes to church twice on Sundays.'

'I wouldn't mention about the allegation of rape if I were you. I'm not sure it's correct. Give me time to verify it,' said MacLeod.

Thomson thought for a while then said, 'I don't like holding back information but I trust your instincts. Ring me as soon as you have something.' As he was leaving he turned and said, 'Who's top of your list?'

'Take your pick. Charlie Steele was my best bet but he's dead.'

'What's stopping him being the murderer and then being bumped off by someone else?' asked Thomson. MacLeod was unimpressed with this suggestion. Steele was a minor player but to humour Thomson he said, 'That will cheer up the team, bringing a dead man in as a suspect is just what we like.' Privately he thought, 'Perhaps we should get out the Ouija board and ask that.'

He debated with himself whether to say it, looked at Thomson and decided against it. Thomson was not noted for his sense of humour.

Fifteen minutes later with MacLeod still in his office, Detective Inspector Reade and Detective Sergeant Milton were going over the 'Things to Do' list. Detective Inspector Janet MacBain and Detective Sergeant Susan Lampart were in another corner of the room carefully going over their notes on the interviews they had conducted with the Reverend Campbell's paramours. Sometimes it is only after an interview is completed that the anomalies appear. Thus a witness could fall neatly into the category of 'suspect' — from innocence to guilt by the stroke of a pen.

Sergeant Gillespie came into the room; he was carrying a large brown paper bag. 'Here's the haversack,' he said, putting the bag on the desk in front of Detective Sergeant Milton. 'It was found beside the wall covered in leaves. I reckon someone covered it in a hurry. It's had the head in it for sometime.'

'What makes you think the head was in it?' asked Reade.

'There are some brown stains on it and it isn't paint. I know it wasn't there when we searched earlier, I personally did that. It's too much of a coincidence: the head appears where we had already searched, and now the haversack turns up at another place, which had been searched. Anyway we will know for sure after it's been to forensic.'

Milton took out a pair of disposable rubber gloves from his desk drawer, and having put them on picked up the haversack and examined it. It was quite new, garish lime green in colour and made of PVC. There were badges from various parts of the country sewn onto the outside of the sack. Edinburgh and Stirling were the only Scots cities. Newcastle, Stratford-upon-Avon and London were amongst the many English towns and cities prominently shown. It seemed that whoever owned the haversack had been on 'the grand tour' of the British Isles. One badge, obscured by bloodstains, showed that the owner had also been in Wales. The badge for Bala, a small town in North Wales, was nearly obliterated by a dark stain.

Sergeant Gillespie's eyes nearly popped out of his head, as he sat down heavily. 'I know who this belongs to.' He was very upset. 'I didn't get a good look at it before, young MacDonald put it in the bag.'

MacLeod joined the group. 'Come on Sergeant, don't keep us in suspense. Who does it belong to?'

'It's young Ewen Jones. My son David, Iain Campbell and Ewen went round Britain. David collected these badges as well. When I picked them up at Buchanan Street Bus Station in Glasgow I remember shuddering at the sight of this haversack; he wouldn't lose it in the dark. We drove home with the windows open; I don't think they had been washed properly for some time.'

Gillespie was beginning to waffle. He didn't want to admit to himself that Ewen had anything to do with any of the murders. His son David was away from home; he had secured a job with the Royal Bank of Scotland and decided not to go to University after his 'Highers'. He was in London and had been there for some months, but Ewen and Iain were at home. 'I'll get the video of Saturday night brought here; you get a TV and video recorder. It's timed so we can see exactly when the boys came to our notice.'

'Thank you. We are going to concentrate on Ewen Jones. He has a lot of questions to answer. He lives only a few hundred yards away,' said MacLeod.

'I thought his mother said she was surprised to see him the morning after the murder.' Milton looked at his notes. 'Yes, here it is, he said he went straight to the party and came home after he had been let out of jail.'

'Perhaps so. It doesn't stop his mother being involved, but somehow I don't think so, I didn't get any vibes from her that she was telling lies but I think it would be foolish not to check her out again.'

MacLeod turned to Detective Inspector MacBain. 'You and Detective Sergeant Lampart go down and see Mrs Jones again. Read her statement and the boy's before you go, check her out. If her son is there leave him alone. We'll bring him in once we are sure of all the facts. He's not going anywhere just yet.'

'Detective Constable MacPherson went over to forensic this morning with the other exhibits. When he comes back I'll get him to take this bag back over there,' said Reade.

MacLeod thought for a second. 'No, we need it quicker than that, get a motorcyclist to get it to them as soon as possible, I have to know whether this is human blood. It doesn't matter if it can't be identified as Campbell's at this stage. I don't want to interview Ewen if this is a hoax by a student, if it is I'll leave it to Sergeant Gillespie. He will really know how to deal with him on that score.'

The preliminary result of the stains showed it was human blood and MacLeod decided that the boy's movements should be looked at on video.

About an hour later MacLeod, Milton, Reade and Sergeant Gillespie were sat watching the video of the surveillance cameras. It was the third time round. They saw Ewen Jones and Iain Campbell coming round the corner from the Argyll Hotel, walking normally and talking in an intimate manner — there was no sign that they were drunk. Ewen looked towards the camera and suddenly pushed Iain. Iain staggered and then picked some rubbish out of the litter bin and threw it at Ewen. Three other youths staggered out of the Crown Hotel laughing and, when they saw Ewen and Iain throwing litter at each other, joined in. It was approximately three minutes later that the police van arrived and all five were placed in the back with little trouble. They were driven to the police station.

'Comments,' said MacLeod.

'They didn't look drunk at first, they seemed to be in deep conversation,' said Milton.

'Aye, and the horseplay looked staged, it was as if they wanted to be arrested. We've been through all the tapes from eight o'clock and this is the first time they are seen in Argyll Street,' said Gillespie.

'Or anywhere else?' queried MacLeod.

'No, nowhere else, only here before they

were arrested,' replied Gillespie.

'Whose party had they been to?' asked Milton.

'They didn't say, but no doubt they will have to say where they were soon.' Gillespie was sure that the boys were in serious trouble. He was praying that he was wrong but it looked bad. He was extremely grateful that his own son was safely away from home with an unshakeable alibi.

'They had plenty of time to do the murder at ten o'clock and get into Dunoon, after all they only appear on the video at ten fifty,' said Reade.

'They don't have a car,' said Gillespie.

'Maybe not but there are plenty of taxis,' said MacLeod. 'Check all the taxi firms, find out who brought them into town.' Gillespie nodded. 'It's likely we have found the murderers,' continued MacLeod, 'but until I've interviewed them no-one is to tell the Detective Superintendent. We want to give him the murderers on a plate, tied up, neat and tidy.' Privately MacLeod was not convinced that these boys were the murderers. He had seen them the morning after Campbell had been found and they were upset but not as upset as they would have been had they perpetrated such a crime.

A young man dressed in a pinstriped suit and carrying a pilot's bag walked into the incident room. He asked, 'Is this the place I have to check out?' Gillespie immediately turned off the video. It was unwise to allow anyone other then the investigating team to see it. Any defence lawyer would have a field day if it were thought that all and sundry were allowed to look at 'evidence'.

MacLeod turned and glared at the youth. 'Forensic I presume?'

The youth flushed. 'I'm Alisdair Sinclair,' he said, 'I should have introduced myself.'

'Alisdair with a 'd',' said Milton.

Sinclair nodded.

'Hm, thought so, no common or garden Alistair for you. This is not the place you have to check out.' Milton stood up and took Alisdair to the window and pointed to a small stone built hut at the far end of the graveyard. 'That is.'

'Could you give me a hint and tell me what I'm looking for?' asked Sinclair.

'Nefarious activity,' said Milton tersely.

Sinclair turned and almost tiptoed out.

'Bit rough on him weren't you?' said MacLeod.

'Not at all,' replied Milton. 'Courtesy costs nothing. He'll learn one day.'

Gillespie switched the video on, once

again. He had rewound the tape whilst young Alisdair had been given his instructions. The team watched the video once more.

Constable Murray came into the room and handed Sergeant Gillespie a note. After reading it he interrupted saying, 'We've found the taxi firm. The boys were picked up at the telephone box in Kilmun and taken to the swimming pool in Dunoon at about ten thirty on Saturday night. The taxi driver and dispatcher are being interviewed now.'

'Once the girls come back and we find out if Mrs Jones has anything to do with this, we'll get the suspects in,' said MacLeod.

Reade asked 'Do you think Mrs Campbell should be seen as well? I think she should be interviewed again.'

MacLeod considered this suggestion. 'Yes, I agree, but I would prefer the boys in custody first. She is a strong woman and I think having her son inside will give us a lever.'

Detective Inspector Janet MacBain and Detective Sergeant Susan Lampart came back to the incident room. 'We've seen Mrs Jones. I'm convinced she knows nothing about the murder of the Reverend Campbell. She didn't know that her son was in Dunoon last Saturday,' said Janet.

'Yes,' said Susan, 'she has given a

statement and, from her demeanour, she had no idea her son had been anywhere near the kirk until the following morning when she met him coming up the path.'

'You two,' said MacLeod, pointing at Detective Inspector Reade and Detective Sergeant Lampart, 'bring in Ewen Jones. You two,' pointing at Detective Inspector MacBain and Detective Sergeant Milton, 'bring in Iain Campbell. I'll meet you at Dunoon police station. It's time the boys were seen properly. They have questions to answer now.'

15

Detective Chief Inspector MacLeod sat in interview room number one at Dunoon police station. In front of him was Ewen Jones. Ewen was frightened; he sat with his hands between his legs, gently rocking backwards and forwards in his seat. He stared down at the table in front of him. Detective Sergeant Lampart sat close to him, close enough to touch him if he needed support. Susan thought, 'He is terrified and it's not us that are giving him the frights.' The tape recorder was running.

MacLeod was thinking that this boy wasn't much older than his eldest girl, Jacqueline. He saw similarity of age in them but couldn't imagine his daughter being interviewed in this way. He wondered what he would do if she ever were. No, comparing this boy with his own family would not do much for his professionalism. He must get on with it.

'Do you know why you are here Ewen?' asked MacLeod.

'Yes, but I didn't kill him, and Iain didn't either.' Ewen said it almost too quickly, without raising his eyes from the desk.

'We know you were in Kilmun last Saturday. You and Iain were picked up by taxi from the telephone kiosk at about ten thirty.'

Ewen looked up. 'Yes.'

MacLeod put his hands on the table heavily in front of Ewen. 'You lied to us, now tell the truth.'

Ewen's eyes filled with tears. 'We didn't kill him, he was already dead.'

'No, but you cut his head off didn't you?'

'No, I didn't, it was Iain, but he didn't kill him. He was already dead, honest Mr MacLeod.' Ewen's voice wavered.

'Why should I believe you?' said MacLeod. 'You had the motive, means and opportunity to kill the Reverend Campbell.'

'Why should I have a motive to do that?' Ewen appeared genuinely puzzled. MacLeod realised that he did not know about his mother and Campbell and decided not to tell him at the moment, but he was circumvented by Detective Sergeant Lampart who told the boy in the cruellest way possible about his mother's secret.

'Surely you know about his affair with your mother?' said Susan Lampart.

Ewen jumped to his feet shouting, 'You're lying. My mother isn't like that.' He lunged towards Detective Sergeant Lampart and MacLeod grabbed him by the shoulders and pushed him hard, making him sit down. Ewen continued shouting and flailing his arms. '*Stop it*,' roared MacLeod.

Ewen calmed down but still muttered, 'It's not true, it's not true.'

'I think you need time to settle so we will put you in the detention room until you calm down.' Susan reached towards Ewen. He pulled away saying, 'Leave me alone, don't touch me.'

'Don't be stupid, she won't hurt you,' said MacLeod. He was upset with Susan for giving away a leverage point so easily. Susan got up and called a uniformed constable into the room. 'Take him away,' MacLeod said. 'We'll see him again when he calms down.'

'Well!' said Susan, 'what do you make of that? I don't think he knew about his mother and Campbell, his reaction to the suggestion was genuine.'

'Yes, very genuine and if you ever give away a leverage point like that again, I will personally wallop you. Never tell anyone anything you know unless you have to. Always get the information from the interviewee, never give it.' MacLeod was not angry but made Susan know he was not very pleased with her.

'Sorry. I'll remember in future.'

MacLeod grunted and said, 'Apart from that, do you think he killed Campbell?'

Susan replied, 'I don't know, I don't think so but I could be wrong. Why didn't you show him the haversack? It was his.'

'Not yet, remember what I have just told you. Keep something back for his final interview. He's too upset at the moment to get any sense out of. Don't rush things, I'm not one to lose a case, I want a suspect to go to court and be found guilty and I want the right person found guilty.' MacLeod had standards: it was better ten guilty people go free than one innocent person go to prison. 'Stay with me while I interview young Iain, I think your education needs expanding.'

Susan agreed, she was learning fast. MacLeod was known as an expert interviewer; she decided to watch, listen and learn as much as she could. She could never do what he did, her personality was totally different, but she could adapt his techniques. She hoped that one day she could have as good a reputation as his.

They were walking along the corridor to go to interview room two when young Alisdair Sinclair walked up the corridor. 'Excuse me Mr MacLeod, I have preliminary findings for you, from that hut you sent me to. Someone has been in there and had sexual intercourse at some time. It appears to have been quite recent, maybe within the last couple of days, no longer. I found traces of semen on the bedclothes. I won't be able to tell you more until I get the results from the swabs. Give me time.'

'How much time do you want? I need the results yesterday,' growled MacLeod.

'I'll get onto it now, it's going to take three to four days minimum. I'm sorry but it's the test itself, I can't hurry it up, honestly.' Sinclair spoke in a pleading manner to MacLeod. His initial youthful arrogance had completely dissipated.

Susan smiled to herself. MacLeod had been a little rough on this young man who didn't realise that MacLeod didn't mean what he said most of the time! But it did take a while to get to know him. She knew he meant what he said to her, but Alisdair had not upset him, only irritated him.

In interview room two young Iain Campbell was nervously sitting quietly, very still like a stone. Detective Sergeant Milton had not spoken a word to him after Detective Inspector Reade had left them alone in the room. Iain had cleared his throat twice in an attempt to speak but found he couldn't. Milton did not encourage the boy to say anything; he had to tell what he knew to MacLeod and only MacLeod.

After Iain had been cautioned again for tape recording purposes MacLeod introduced himself and Detective Sergeants Milton and Lampart. 'We have been told that you cut your father's head off,' said MacLeod.

Iain opened his mouth to speak but no sound came out. He tried again, but his eyes glazed over and he fainted with a thump onto the small desk in front of him. 'Oh no!' sighed MacLeod. 'Somehow I don't think we are going to get very far today.'

Milton and Lampart both jumped up from their seats. Milton held Iain up while Susan unloosened his shirt collar. Iain's face was a grey white colour, his breathing was shallow, and he was in a deep faint, he was not acting. For the tape recorder MacLeod said, 'Iain Campbell has fainted, I will be sending for a doctor.' He switched the machine off. He looked at the now recovering youth. 'Wimp! At your age I was fighting for Queen and country, not fainting at the first sign of trouble.' He had more time for Ewen, who had reacted violently at the suggestion that his mother was not 'pure', than this boy who had fainted at the first sign of trouble. He did not know how he had had the courage to mutilate his father's body.

In the conference room later MacLeod said to Milton. 'I hope the doctor gets that young man brought round soon.'

Milton replied, 'Susan seems to think he's OK now, but she's staying with him. He seems to be getting a good rapport with her, I thought it best she looked after him until the doctor has finished.'

'If he faints when I speak to him, how on earth could he murder his father and then cut off his head?' said MacLeod.

'I don't know, neither of them seem capable of killing a fly, never mind the Reverend Campbell and then doing that to him,' said Milton.

Just then Detective Inspector Reade came into the room. 'Excuse me Sir, but Mr James Balfour is here, he says he is representing the boys and would like to have a word with you.'

'I'll come out and see him.' MacLeod got out of his chair; he was pleased something else could occupy his mind. Dwelling on young Iain's future was beginning to depress him. James Balfour was in the waiting room. 'Good morning Mr Balfour, how may I help you?' said MacLeod.

'What line is your investigation taking?' asked Balfour.

'You know very well I can't tell you,

you will have to see the Fiscal,' replied MacLeod.

'I know that, but I think you could help me. I would like to sit in on their interviews,' said Balfour.

'No, I'm not allowing that. If you want to take it up with the Fiscal, go ahead. Why do you want to sit in anyway? You know very well it isn't allowed.' MacLeod was totally bemused. It was only the second time in his career that a defence lawyer had made this request. Scottish and English law were so different. In Scotland there is no right for lawyers to sit in with their clients, nor do clients have the right to have a lawyer present whilst they are being interviewed.

'I suppose I'll have to see the Fiscal before I can see the boys too?' queried Balfour.

'What's up with you? You know all this, why are you so anxious?' MacLeod was curious.

'I've been asked by both their mothers to look after them, and you know what mothers are like. I can't go back to them without at least asking you,' said Balfour in a matter of fact tone.

'I understand, you can tell them the boys are fine. I'll treat them as if they were my own, I always do,' replied MacLeod.

After Balfour left MacLeod contemplated

the interviews with the boys and everyone involved with Campbell. He was becoming annoyed at the slow progress and could be very impatient when he felt he was being thwarted or the investigation was not proceeding fast enough. MacLeod also had a gut feeling that Ewen was telling the truth: the boys had not murdered the Reverend. The story that young Iain had cut his own father's head off was too strange not to be true. But who had wound this timorous young man up to the extent that all normal feelings were thrown out of the window? Ewen seemed the stronger of the two and he decided that he would be interviewed once again, but not now. There were other fish to fry.

MacLeod rang Duncan Grey and told him where the investigation was going; it was his duty to do so.

'I don't believe it. I've known those boys since they were babies, they couldn't have done it,' said Grey.

'You may have known them a long time but they have admitted decapitating Campbell, though only after his death. They were there shortly after he was murdered, if not at the time. I'm afraid they are definitely involved. I think they should be charged with mutilation of the body until we have more evidence.'

'Not yet, interview them again and tell me what happens. I appreciate young Iain is in shock but he should be OK after the doctor has seen him,' said Grey.

'No. Now would not be a good time, I would like to leave them for a couple of hours. I have other enquiries to make,' MacLeod insisted.

'Can you tell me what 'other enquiries'?' asked Grey.

'Only details,' replied MacLeod.

'I know you and your details, sometimes they are more important than anything you tell me,' said Grey.

MacLeod decided it was time to change the subject. 'By the way, I had James Balfour in. He said he was defending the boys, and asked if he could sit in with the interviews.'

'What! Not a chance, he's been watching too much television. He knows very well he can't.' Grey was shocked.

'No doubt you will tell him that when he sees you.' MacLeod was now smiling to himself. He knew what Grey would be saying to Balfour.

'He wouldn't ask me, it's against all rules and regulations. If he tries to impose on our friendship I'll lose another friend!' Grey was now talking through gritted teeth.

'I thought that was how you would react,' MacLeod said, 'but don't get too upset, he promised their mothers he would do everything he could for them. I believe he is on his way to you now. Will you see him and be polite?'

Grey sighed, 'All right but only for you. By the way, what 'details' were you talking about?' He was not so easily put off.

'I'll keep you informed on my 'details'. I need to sort out some things before I see the boys again. I promise,' said MacLeod.

'Have you told the Superintendent yet?' asked Grey.

'Not yet, I'll tell him when the time comes. Bye.' MacLeod put down the phone; he didn't want to get into any further discussions with the Fiscal.

MacLeod called Detective Inspector Janet MacBain to his office. 'I need you and Detective Sergeant Lampart to do two things for me. First, I want to know where Mr James Balfour's wife is; second, I want you to see Mrs Campbell. She hasn't been questioned about her relationship with her husband. You brought in her son Iain, use your feminine touch to really get to know her. I think she holds the key to all this. I don't believe we really have the real motive for Campbell's murder.'

'What about Steele's murder?' asked Janet.

'One will lead us to the other,' replied MacLeod.

After the detectives had left he said to Detective Inspector Reade, 'I want you to find Campbell's previous parish. Ask Morris, he'll find it on his computer if he hasn't already, and speak to the present incumbent. Also speak to the church elders and find out why he left, whether it was voluntary or whether he was pushed. I need to know. You may have some difficulty there, but try anyway.'

'I think he came from Glasgow. His wife could tell us,' replied Reade.

'No doubt she could but I don't want her to know we are making these enquiries; asking her could prove unproductive. Detective Inspector MacBain and Detective Sergeant Lampart are dealing with that side of the investigation. I need you to do this.'

Later he was with Detective Sergeant Milton in the car heading towards the home of James Balfour. Milton had already found out that Balfour had left the police station and told his secretary that he was on his way home.

'What's up, Boss?' Milton knew MacLeod's moods. He was happy and seemed relieved.

'I've worked it out I think. But not quite,

I'll know better after we see Balfour. This is a pre-meditated murder, it's been planned for some time. At least six months or so. The boys came home on impulse. They should have been away from home but weren't, so I know they did not kill him. I don't know whether they mutilated the body or not. They are shielding someone, after today I hope the pieces fall together. Let's get to Balfour quickly. I have a gut feeling that something is very wrong.'

16

Detective Inspector Janet MacBain and Detective Sergeant Susan Lampart were sitting in Susan's car outside the late Reverend William Campbell's home. 'I'm not happy about this,' said Janet. 'Use your feminine touch, he said, find out about their relationship, he said. Now what kind of reaction are we going to get? I only lifted her son a few hours ago and he expects us to get intimate and personal information out of her?'

'I know,' said Susan. 'But what else can we do? You know Mr MacLeod, if he wants information we have to get it, I do feel sorry for Mrs Campbell. Her husband dead and her son arrested. It's not her week.'

'Nor ours,' sighed Janet. 'Oh well, let's get on with it.'

'Not to be pushy or anything but I think I should take the lead on this one, she may respond better to me. I would in her shoes,' said Susan.

'So would I; it's a very good idea you taking the lead. I'll try to keep in the background as much as possible,' replied

Janet. She was not looking forward to this at all.

As they walked up the gravel path to the front door of the Manse, their feet crunched the red stones; the sound they made underfoot seemed to echo in their ears. The heavy door was flung open before they had time to knock and Mrs Julia Campbell stood there. She had her arms folded protectively in front of her. Glaring at the two detectives she demanded, 'What do you want now?'

'Only a couple of questions,' said Susan. 'We really need to see you now. Wouldn't it be better if we came in rather than stand on the doorstep?'

Mrs Campbell hesitated and seemed to consider whether she should let these two in the house. 'Yes, I suppose so.'

Susan and Janet picked their way carefully past the maze of packed boxes in the hallway and went into the lounge. Julia noted there were dirty, empty cups and glasses on the table. WPC O'Neill was a tidy person and would not have left one cup unwashed.

'Where's the policewoman?' asked Janet.

'You don't think I wanted anyone from your lot in my house after you took my son, I sent her away. Now less of the chit-chat, why are you here?'

Julia sat down heavily in the chair next to the fireplace. The fire had long gone out and ashes spilled over onto the hearth. Julia was usually careful at all times to keep the house tidy. Being the wife of the minister with people popping in and out, day and night, to see him made her keep up appearances. Since being told of her husband's death she didn't care what anything looked like, it seemed unimportant somehow. Deep down she was relieved that she didn't have to do anything that she didn't want to.

Susan decided to be direct. 'I'm afraid we need some information about your marriage.'

She did not have time to go any further, for Julia interrupted her with venom. 'You have taken my son, my husband's personal papers, searched my home and even asked me for samples of his fingerprints on any personal items. Why you should want his fingerprints I will never know. And I'm sure Margaret O'Neill would be able to tell you we had separate bedrooms, after all she was the one who snooped around the house. Now you want to know the state of my marriage. Well there wasn't one.' She almost shouted the last sentence and collapsed back into her chair.

Susan regretted that Mrs Campbell had

sent the policewoman away on two counts: first, O'Neill had a good rapport with the widow and second, on a selfish note, it would have made the interview much easier if she had been around. 'You know we have a job to do and unfortunately your son is involved,' said Susan.

'He didn't kill his father,' Julia spat the words out. 'I know my boy and he wouldn't do such a thing.'

'We know he was at the kirk that night, he has already told us that,' said Janet.

Her sympathy for this woman was receding. Janet had no time for anyone who did not face facts, no matter how unpalatable they may be, and Julia was the kind of woman who had an ideal world in her head and anything that didn't fit was conveniently ignored. She felt an irritation that was becoming hard to control and not show, but she knew if she did show her feelings this interview would be fated. Julia would simply clam up and they would never get what Mr MacLeod needed.

Julia suddenly looked up at the ceiling and clutched her chest. Her breathing became shallow, her face drained of colour. Janet immediately regretted the uncharitable thoughts and concern spread through her like a wave. She got up and went towards

Julia who gave a moan and fell forward into her arms.

'Oh my God, she's having a heart attack. Quick Susan, ring for an ambulance.' Janet dragged Julia as gently as she could from the chair and lay her on the floor on her side. She pulled the cushion from the chair and propped her up. Whilst kneeling beside her she placed her fingers on her neck and felt her pulse at the carotid artery. It was weak and fast. Her colour was a pallid blue and as she lay there breathing shallowly the colour changed and she returned almost to normality.

Susan hurried back to Janet saying, 'The ambulance is on it's way. What did I do? I didn't lean on her.' She sounded distraught.

'Nothing,' replied Janet. 'I think Mrs Campbell has taken a bad turn because of everything that has happened. You know the body can only take so much. It wasn't your fault.'

Julia began to come round and tried to get up. 'Don't move,' commanded Janet. 'We've sent for an ambulance.'

Julia had a dazed look on her face and after a moment's rest she appeared to become aware of her surroundings. She grasped Janet's arm with a surprisingly strong grip and said in short bursts of words, in obvious pain, 'I killed him. I did it. He was having affairs. All through our married life. From one to another. Let my son go.'

Janet prised Julia's fingers apart and released her arm. 'I don't think you did. Now relax.'

She carefully put Julia's arm down. Julia clasped Janet's fingers and said, 'I did it, I tell you. I killed him.'

She was so agitated that Janet said, more to calm her down than with any conviction, 'Yes, all right, I believe you. Now settle down and don't make the situation worse.'

Julia relaxed and closed her eyes. She said quietly, 'Remember what I have said. I killed my husband.' Her breathing became shallow and Janet checked her pulse again. It was stronger than before but still irregular.

The paramedics arrived within minutes. They were two men in their late thirties. They had an air of total efficiency which greatly comforted both Janet and Susan. All police officers are trained in First Aid and can assist in saving lives, but the training does not give most officers total confidence in their own abilities. They are always relieved to see the professionals arrive at the scene of any accident or emergency.

Janet was pleased to stand back and

allow the paramedics space to get on with their job. Fortunately for Julia, they had great experience in the management of heart attacks and their quiet efficiency was impressive. Julia was lifted onto a stretcher and wheeled to the ambulance. An oxygen mask was put over her face; her breath instantly misted up the clear plastic.

Geoff the senior man said to Janet, who was hovering anxiously round the open doors of the ambulance, 'Who put her on the floor and looked after her?'

Janet panicked a little. She thought she had done something wrong. 'I did.' He smiled at the fear on her face. 'You did the right thing and I suspect you saved her life. It's a good job you were here.'

Janet exhaled with relief. She felt as if she had held her breath from the time that Julia had collapsed and now she could breathe properly again.

The ambulance left with blue lamps flashing but no sirens blaring. It was for Julia's benefit so that she would not be unduly disturbed by the sirens, which would not help her condition. Susan watched the ambulance go and said a silent prayer for Julia. She was not particularly religious but felt her prayers might help; they wouldn't do any harm anyway. A feeling of guilt swept over her. 'It's silly, I didn't do it to her,' she thought, but somehow she felt responsible and fervently asked her God to help. The family had been intact a few days ago, but now husband was murdered, wife was on her way to intensive care and son was in custody. What else could go wrong for them?

'She didn't kill him,' Susan said to Janet, 'and she knew she was having a heart attack and was trying to protect her son.'

Janet said nothing; she was struggling with the rising suspicion in her mind that Mrs Julia Campbell was not what she seemed. There was something about the strength of the hands that had gripped her which made her believe something else. Yes, she had had a heart attack, of that there was no doubt, but there was something not quite right, which she couldn't put into words. Finally she said, 'Ring Mr MacLeod and tell him what has happened. I'm going to go to the neighbours, I need to talk to them.'

Susan looked at Janet and was about to say something, but the look on her face was enough to stop her. 'All right, do you want me to stay here and wait for you?

'Yes, but have a quiet look around, you never know, something may have been missed. Margaret O'Neill is very efficient, however she may have overlooked something. Look in the bathroom cabinet, she may have medication or something. You never know what you might find.'

Susan rang the Detective Chief Inspector's mobile and gave him the news of Julia's illness. He said, 'Thanks for telling me. We are at James Balfour's home at the moment, but there's no-one in, and we need to see him urgently. When you get back to the office see if you can find out where he may be.'

'Detective Inspector MacBain has gone next door to see the neighbours. I don't know when she will be back, she's told me to have a look round the house.'

MacLeod was now intrigued. 'Janet must think she's on to something,' he thought. 'Why is she doing that?' he asked Susan.

'I've no idea. She just went off.'

'All right, have a look round and both of you report back to me at the office when you're finished. You have half an hour at the most.' MacLeod ended the call.

Milton had overheard the conversation. He thought for a few seconds then said, 'You know, I trust Detective Inspector MacBain's instincts, she may get something you need, you shouldn't have given them a deadline.'

'Shouldn't have given a deadline. You know as well as I do those women will ignore it if they are on to something, but it is nice to feel I am the boss sometimes,' said MacLeod.

★ ★ ★

Susan started looking in the rooms starting at the top floor. She felt a little uncomfortable, especially as Mrs Campbell had been taken to hospital and there was no-one else in the large rattling house. Every floorboard seemed to creak in protest.

The top floor was an attic converted into three small rooms. Each room had a small bed and wardrobe with matching dressing table. The furniture was covered with dust sheets. This was the floor where the servants lived when the Manse was inhabited by far richer ministers than today's incumbent.

Susan saw that one of the rooms had a small and threadbare carpet, unlike the other rooms which had bare wooden floors. 'Obviously the housekeeper's room,' she thought. 'I expect I would have been a kitchen maid in a past life. I would have drawn the short straw.'

She went to the next floor down and on into each bedroom in succession. There were five in total but only three seemed to be used. One was obviously Iain's. Although nearly everything had been packed there were signs of Blu-Tac on the wall where posters had been carelessly attached. The bed was unmade and the wardrobe was wide open. Coat hangars were empty and on the floor were two pairs of jeans, three dirty T-shirts and a pair of trainer type boots that needed a good wash, never mind a brush over. The smell of sweaty socks pervaded the air. 'I'll bet his mum was glad when he went to University. If this is the state of his room when everything has been packed, then I'm glad I never saw it when he lived at home,' thought Susan.

The next room she went into appeared to belong to William Campbell, and he was the sole occupant. There was a single bed with a completely bare mattress visible, no sheets or pillow cases. The wardrobe contained a jogging suit and the top drawer contained two pairs of socks and one pair of stripy boxer shorts. There was nothing on the bedside table.

The master bedroom, obviously Mrs Campbell's room, contained a double bed which was made up with a striped duvet cover and matching pillow cases. The wardrobe contained her clothes and likewise the drawers were still full of her underwear, jumpers and casual wear. On the bedside table were three bottles of pills. Susan examined them and saw that they had been dispensed by Boots the Chemist in Dunoon. She could not understand what the pills were for, but sensing that the hospital would need to know what medication Mrs Campbell was on, she made a note of the drugs and put them into her pocket, intending to get them to the hospital as soon as possible.

She returned downstairs and found the ground floor devoid of any signs of habitation by the Campbell family. All personal items had been packed except for a few cups and saucers in the kitchen, and the usual tea and coffee makings. Even the fridge contained only half a pint of milk and the usual piece of 'mousetrap' cheese.

Susan remembered Janet's instruction to look in the bathroom. She opened the white cabinet and saw nothing. No pills, potions or talcum powder. She looked around for a shaving kit. Her memory of William Campbell's head — she shuddered at the vision — told her that he was clean-shaven.

Wondering where his toiletries were she searched his room again. Nothing. She searched the bin in the kitchen; it contained a few tea bags and a sugar bag. She walked outside to the yard and saw a 'wheelie bin'. 'I hope it isn't full,' she thought. When she lifted the lid she was relieved to see it only had one small plastic bag in it. Not being tall enough to reach Susan tipped the bin forward and grabbed the bag. Carefully opening it she saw it was full of the Reverend William Campbell's toiletries, shaving kit, after-shave and deodorant. Taking the bag back into the kitchen she sat down and waited for Janet to return.

17

Janet knocked on the door of a detached cottage next door to the Manse; she looked to her left and saw that a wall some four feet in height separated the two properties. The wall was not of brick but irregular grey stone typical of the area. It was well maintained, though it had a wire and mesh fence atop of it, which completely detracted from its rugged beauty.

A small child opened the door; she was about five years old and had a trusting face. 'My Mummy will be here in a minute, she is in the bathroom. Who are you?' From behind her a harassed young woman appeared. She was in her early twenties, slim, pretty and wearing a white T-shirt and dark blue leggings. She had a figure that Janet would have given her eyeteeth for.

'Ellen,' she said, 'you know you shouldn't open the door.' She gently took hold of the child's arm and pulled her back into the house, and with the other hand started to shut the door. Looking up she became even more flustered when she saw Janet MacBain. 'Sorry, I didn't hear you,' said Lorna Burns.

'I know. You were in the bathroom,' Janet said with a smile on her face and in her voice.

Lorna blushed. 'Ellen!' she exclaimed and gave her daughter a stern look. Ellen looked at her, tears welling in her eyes, dewdrops quivering on eyelids.

'No! Don't scold her, she was very polite and didn't do anything wrong.' Janet loved children and had no desire to have any of her own, but she hated to see them upset for no reason. It broke her heart when she had to deal with abused children who had had their innocence ripped away by selfish perverts. The perverts knew what they did but had no desire to exert a small amount of willpower to control their ugly urges to inflict pain on others. She regarded them as cowards and no amount of persuasion could convince her they had any excuse for doing what they did. She thought that they should be locked up forever when children were involved. Janet had no sympathy for paedophiles whatsoever, and the excuses they always gave, that it wasn't their fault because the children had seduced them, made her furious.

After Janet had introduced herself, Lorna invited her into the home; this was most definitely a home rather than a house. The contrast between the Manse and this house next door was as different as chalk and cheese. They went into a bright kitchen, recently modernised, where a wonderful smell of fresh baking made Janet inwardly groan. She knew that if offered cake she would not be able to refuse. The house felt bright and cheery, Ellen was sent into the living room to play and a couple of minutes later Janet was settled at the kitchen table with a steaming cup of coffee and two iced fairy cakes in front of her.

'Could I ask you some questions about your neighbour, Mrs Campbell?' Janet was direct.

Lorna stiffened and said, 'What is it exactly you want to know? I feel sorry for her I suppose. I did like Mr Campbell, he always passed the time of day and he didn't deserve to die like that.'

'Come on Lorna, you are changing the subject. I want to know about Mrs Campbell not the Reverend. I know you haven't been round to see her, in fact she has had very few callers. The WPC has kept a record of visitors, but it's very sparse. I also noticed the wall has a wire fence on it. What was she like?'

Lorna hesitated and thought for a few seconds before she said, 'I wouldn't spit

240

on her if she was on fire. She's the only person I've met I could honestly say I hate. I wouldn't set foot in her house. My husband had to put the fence up to stop Ellen throwing her toys over the wall because Mrs Campbell complained about it. She ripped one of Ellen's dollies apart, then give it back to her telling her that she would burn it next time, Ellen was distraught. When I tackled her about it she put on her sweet face and said that I was mad to believe she had done such a thing. Unfortunately for her I saw her do it from my kitchen window.'

Lorna stopped talking. She was angry; her hands were agitated as if they had a life of their own, first waving this way, then that. She gained control of herself and glanced at Janet's plate: only empty fluted cake casings lay abandoned on it. 'Would you like another cake?' she asked.

Janet looked down at the plate. Not a crumb was left; she had eaten the cakes absent-mindedly, in fact she didn't remember eating the cakes at all. Guilt washed over her and she refused the offer with thanks.

Lorna didn't wait for any encouragement to carry on her description of her neighbour. 'She is a nasty evil woman, but she gives the impression that butter wouldn't melt in her mouth. Everyone was taken in by her at first, but when her true nature came out I thought she was possessed by the devil. I don't know how that poor man put up with her. I've lived next door to her for eight years and it wasn't until I stayed at home when I had Claire that I found out about her. All the neighbours round here have had a run-in with her at one time or another. Once she starts she has a vendetta against that one person, the only relief is that you know she will go on to someone else sooner or later. The worst thing is that I didn't believe the others when they told me. She was so nice to me at first. We can only cope by completely ignoring her.'

'Does that include now?' asked Janet.

'Especially now. She would take it as a weakness if I went round to see her, even though it's what a normal neighbour would do. She would get great pleasure by trying to destroy us afterwards.' Lorna hated no-one in the world, and felt some sympathy for Mrs Campbell's future. She did not have to be a clairvoyant to know how lonely she would be when she got old, but she hated her right now.

'But she is moving on, how could she do anything?' said Janet.

'Easy, as soon as we went in she would be fine for some time then find a reason to throw us out. She has a nasty turn of phrase and she follows it up with letters. I burned the one she sent to my husband. She accused me of having an affair with Mr Campbell, and she went into graphic detail too. She even said that Ellen was not my husband's.' Lorna bristled. 'That was one of her mild ones. Every time she did anything she always said she was sorry and it was her pills that caused it. She is on anti-depressants and has some for angina. I suppose she stopped taking them and had an attack. She always wants to be the centre of attention, there's something not right there.'

Janet stiffened. 'Do you mean that she deliberately stopped taking her pills to have a heart attack?'

Lorna replied, 'That's exactly what I mean, she's done it before.'

Janet was stunned. 'But she could have died.'

Lorna replied, 'Not her, only the good die young, the devil looks after his own.' She tapped her head. 'She seems happy only when someone feels sorry for her or she is causing pain.'

Janet interrupted: 'What kind of pain?'

Lorna realised what she had said. 'I don't mean she could have killed her husband. She gets her kicks from inflicting sorrow on someone. She likes to see grief on their faces.

If you are thinking that she could have killed her husband, then I know she couldn't do that. The one thing I do know is that she loved him and if she was going to kill him she would have done it years ago.'

Janet thought about it. 'If he was leaving her, perhaps she could.'

Lorna was adamant. 'No. She would have been in her element, she would have hounded him and anyone he went with. She would rather destroy his life than cause his death. Think of the sympathy she would have received if he had left her. We were planning a 'Hurrah She's Gone' party for next weekend. She's spoiled that now.' Lorna was glum.

Janet had been taking a few notes whilst Lorna had been talking. She looked at her pad and realised she had missed a vital question due to her fascination at Lorna's revelations about Julia Campbell's character. She asked, 'How did you know that Mrs Campbell sent the letter to your husband?'

'She signed it of course, I'll give her that. If she was going to say something she would always make sure you knew exactly where the accusation came from,' said Lorna.

'Did you ever do anything about it?'

'You mean by suing her for libel. No way, she was the minister's wife and who would hurt the poor man; it would have destroyed his career. No matter how angry you were, it would have been wrong to do it to him,' said Lorna.

'Do you happen to remember last Saturday Night? Did Mrs Campbell go out?' asked Janet.

'I wouldn't really know but I don't think so. I can hear the car, the garage is just over the fence. I didn't hear it on Saturday. I saw Mr Campbell go out earlier, he was walking, he liked to walk you know. He waved to me as he passed the window.'

The overall impression that Lorna gave of Mrs Campbell was the neighbour from Hell. She complained about everything, in fact it seemed that she was known as a harridan. 'Now why didn't anyone tell us this before?' Janet was bemused.

'It's quite simple, she has lost her husband and no-one here believes she could have killed him. Another thing, you didn't ask. If you are thinking of going round the neighbours may I suggest you don't go to Mrs Stephens on the other side. If you mention Mrs Campbell's name she will throw you out of the house. She's lived in that house for forty years and has had nothing but trouble with Mrs Campbell since she came here.'

Janet decided to broach the subject of the alleged rape committed by William Campbell. 'Not that,' said Lorna. 'It was supposed to be me. Mr Campbell came round here and visited us; my husband was home too. Within half an hour she was round telling me to report him for raping me. We were gobsmacked. The next thing I knew I was asked about it at the local shop. I don't know why anyone would believe it of him. He wasn't that kind of man.'

Janet thanked Lorna for her help and as she was leaving the house Lorna said, 'Oh, there is one other thing. Have you noticed that her three daughters haven't visited? She accused them of having sex with their own father last time they were over and they haven't been back since. I overheard the argument. It was lucky that Mr Campbell wasn't around, I think he would have left her there and then. I don't think he really knew what she was like, you see he was such a nice man no-one wanted to upset him by complaining.'

Janet went back to the Manse and met Susan as she came out of the house. 'I've rung the station,' she said. 'They are sending someone over with Iain's keys to lock up. They won't be here for half an hour; it should be all right to leave. No-one will take anything.'

Susan showed Janet the tablets she had found and suggested they take them to the hospital before going back to the office. Janet shook her head and said, 'I think we should hang on to them, but we'll tell the hospital what medication she is on.' Susan then showed Janet the plastic bag she had retrieved from the 'wheelie bin'. 'It looks like she was getting rid of anything to do with him already,' said Janet.

On the way back to the office to meet the Detective Chief Inspector, Janet told Susan what Mrs Stephens had said.

'I don't believe it,' said Susan. 'Mrs Campbell doesn't appear to be like that. I don't want to believe it. Do you think she could have murdered her husband?'

'I don't know. If she did then it would explain why Iain cut his father's head off: he was trying to point the finger of suspicion elsewhere. Or she got him so upset about his father that reason went out of the window and he was furious someone had killed his father before he did,' said Janet.

'She couldn't have murdered Charlie Steele. WPC O'Neill was with her when that murder was committed,' said Susan.

'Right, but where was Iain? He was with

Ewen in his mother's car, that's where. We haven't questioned him about that, yet,' said Janet.

★ ★ ★

Detective Chief Inspector MacLeod was sitting in the office in the incident room with Detective Sergeant Milton. He was agitated having just received the report from Janet. Most murders are domestics as he well knew and had he had Mrs Campbell's background thoroughly investigated she would not be in hospital now, out of reach of interview, surrounded by a protective ring of doctors and nurses. He had been told that he would not be able to see her for some time. He mentally chastised himself for allowing his natural sympathy for a victim's wife to overcome his professional conduct.

'Too long,' he muttered, 'I need to know what her movements were recently, and what she had said and to whom.'

'Excuse me,' said Milton, 'what did you say?'

'Nothing, John. I'm angry with myself that's all. I feel that something else is going to happen and it will be my fault if anyone else is hurt.'

'Don't be silly, you weren't to know. I

248

saw her too and I cannot believe that this woman could have had anything to do with the murder. If anyone should have seen it I should, after all I was the observer,' said Milton.

'I'm not convinced, however I'll put it down to experience. Two other things, I don't want the boys interviewed about Charlie Steele just yet and I want Balfour found. I don't care how many man hours it takes, I want him,' said MacLeod.

'Why? Surely you haven't put him on the list. He's a lawyer,' said Milton.

'He holds the key, I know he does and I need to speak to him,' said MacLeod.

Detective Inspector Reade came into the room. 'I've had the Glasgow police go round to the last place Campbell worked: he was moved on because he was supposedly having an affair with one of the congregation. The strange thing is that his wife reported him: she wrote a letter to the diocese and told them everything. Apparently he was such a good minister they felt that it was a one-off and he was sent on to another ministry. The woman involved committed suicide after the Campbells left.'

'Don't tell me, she hung herself,' said MacLeod.

'Wrong, she took poison. She left a note

saying that it wasn't because Campbell had left her. He had talked her out of it months before and made her feel good about herself. Unfortunately she became depressed again after they left. She did it about a year later, so it couldn't be connected with Campbell.'

'I'm pleased in a way. I'd hate to find out that Mrs Campbell was a serial killer,' said MacLeod.

The door was pushed open and Detective Superintendent Thomson swept into the room. 'I'm back,' he said.

'I can see that, always one for stating the obvious,' thought MacLeod. 'Have you frightened my staff to death again?' he asked aloud.

'Not at all, I'm not like that, I came to see if I can do anything. I sense that you are getting somewhere and you know I like to be in on the kill,' said Thomson.

'Unfortunate turn of phrase in this case. Yes and no really,' said MacLeod. He brought Thomson up to date.

'Perhaps Mrs Campbell should be seen now,' said Thomson.

'I would but she is in intensive care and it would be easier getting one past you than the hospital staff,' MacLeod commented with tongue in cheek.

Thomson preened, he was never averse

to flattery and said, 'I'll go to the hospital, you never know; I'll take Detective Inspector MacBain with me.' He left in his usual rushed manner shouting, 'Get your kit MacBain, you are coming with me.'

Janet looked startled and got to her feet almost knocking the chair over. She followed him in a hurry.

'Nice one, Boss. You got him out of our hair,' said Reade.

'Don't know what you mean.' MacLeod feigned innocence.

'I bet Janet will have something to say when she gets back,' said Reade.

MacLeod said, 'I cannot believe that William Campbell didn't know about his wife. He must have known.'

Milton replied, 'Not necessarily if no-one told him, how is he supposed to know? If she was Mrs Nice Face at home and Mrs Nasty outside it would be easy for her to keep the real self from him.' MacLeod thought about his relationship with his wife; she couldn't deceive him that way. Milton went on, 'Don't forget, she isn't normal if she is like that. You can't judge normal against abnormal.' MacLeod grunted, not convinced.

Detective Constable Morris put his head round the corner of the door saying, 'Mr

Balfour has been seen, he went into his house about five minutes ago. He's not answering the door.' 'Come on John, lets go.' MacLeod was at the door quickly, Detective Sergeant Milton hot on his heels.

18

As Detective Chief Inspector MacLeod and Detective Sergeant Milton arrived at the home of James Balfour, Constable Anderson stopped them at the gate. He looked flustered.

'Don't go any further Sir, I've sent for the Sergeant.'

'It must be serious if you have sent for the Sergeant.' Milton was a little sarcastic.

MacLeod dug him in the ribs. He did not approve of discourtesy, he found it unproductive. It tended to push self-conscious officers into a shell and the overconfident ones took offence and refused to communicate. Either way the object of such sarcasm became uncooperative.

'Go on, son, tell me what happened.' Anderson gave MacLeod a relieved look. He was pleased to see an officer of a rank higher than himself on the scene; he could now happily hand over responsibility for a totally unfamiliar situation.

'It's Mr Balfour, Sir, he's in the house but when I knocked on the door he waved a shotgun out of an upstairs window and told me to go away or he would shoot.'

MacLeod groaned inwardly. He only wanted to talk to Balfour; he did not need to be involved in any histrionics. These grand gestures irritated him; it spoiled his sense of order.

'OK, you stay with Detective Sergeant Milton in the car, I will go to the house and see what I can do,' said MacLeod. Milton became alarmed.

'No Sir, you can't do that, he is armed and dangerous. You know we have to wait for the task force and the trained negotiators.' He feared for MacLeod's safety. He held his arm in an ineffective attempt to stop him approaching the house.

'Yes, I can do this. I should have seen his state of mind before and done something about it. He is armed but I don't believe he is dangerous. I won't be long. If the cavalry arrive hold them off until I get back, I don't want to lose him to a shoot-out at the OK Corral. Anyway if you remember I'm the trained negotiator for this area. If anyone asks I'm just getting a head start. I'll take the mobile but don't ring me I'll ring you if necessary.'

MacLeod walked steadily to the front door without any rush. When he was about three feet from the door, the upstairs window opened and James Balfour shouted out of the window. 'Go away or I'll shoot.' He was brandishing a shotgun.

MacLeod shouted up to him, 'I need to talk to you, and I would like to do it before the armed police officers arrive. You know they are on the way, all I want is for this to be sorted without anyone getting hurt.' 'Especially me,' he thought offering up a prayer to his guardian angel. 'I wouldn't be here if I didn't know you are not a violent man at heart. I trust you.' MacLeod handed his well-being over to Balfour. In any other situation he would not have approached the gunman in this manner, but every situation is different and he thought he knew this man. MacLeod felt that Balfour was trying to decide whether he should kill himself, not harm anyone else.

As MacLeod waited patiently, he heard sirens. The cavalry were on the way. Balfour seemed to make his mind up when he heard the wail of the emergency services, came downstairs, opened the door and, still holding the shotgun, beckoned MacLeod to enter. His face was ashen and contorted in pain; his soul was in torment. As MacLeod walked through the door, he heard Thomson's familiar voice. Thomson shouted something which MacLeod chose to ignore — he continued on his way.

Thomson had decided to call in at Dunoon police station before going to the hospital just in time to hear about the siege at Balfour's house. Janet told him that MacLeod was on his way to the locus as he was anxious to see Balfour. Thomson knew that MacLeod would ignore 'standing orders' if necessary; his maxim was that 'rules are for the guidance of wise men and the blind obedience of fools.' Thomson drove to the house following a police car with sirens blaring and blue lights flashing. Janet was terrified, she seriously doubted that Thomson was doing anything other than pointing the car in the direction he was looking. He didn't seem to drive it and she hoped that he didn't turn to say anything to her or they would end up in a ditch. When they arrived they were just in time to see MacLeod walk into the house. Thomson shouted for him to stop, but either he didn't hear or ignored the order.

Janet walked over to Detective Sergeant Milton who looked at her and said, 'You look as if you have seen a ghost, or has his driving stayed the same?'

'His driving, it was bad enough when we were on our way to the station, but when he is in a hurry . . . ' She stopped without finishing the sentence, sensing Thomson at her shoulder. Milton nodded; he had some experience of Thomson's driving and sympathised but refrained from commenting within his hearing.

'Why didn't you stop him?' demanded Thomson of Milton.

'I tried Sir, as this young man here can vouch,' he said, indicating Constable Anderson, who was trying to make himself inconspicuous, 'but he was determined to talk to Balfour and, as he pointed out, he is a trained negotiator. It's his decision how the incident should be managed.'

Thomson grunted and walked off. He went to see Sergeant Gillespie who had arrived some minutes before him in the noisy police car. 'Have you sent for the armed officers, Sergeant?'

'Not yet, I wanted to assess the situation first, I don't like to call them out unless it is absolutely necessary. They have to come from Glasgow and it's going to take some time. I know Mr Balfour well, and I think he must have had a breakdown, he's usually a mild-mannered man. I can't understand what is going on.' Gillespie was bemused by the whole situation.

Thomson said, 'Put the armed officers on stand-by at least. If anything happens to Mr MacLeod because we haven't called them I'll carry the can, but you will know about it from me.' He prodded his finger in Gillespie's chest.

'I'll get on to it,' Gillespie replied, whose private thoughts consisted mainly of swear words at this arrogant interloper. He respected Thomson but did not like him.

Thomson rang Force Headquarters on his mobile phone and gave the Assistant Chief Constable an update on the incident. To Gillespie's surprise he said that *he* had only now decided to put armed officers on standby and that MacLeod was in the house on his authority, actively negotiating with the man.

'He has covered me and if anything happens to Mr MacLeod I suspect that Mr Thomson will be lucky to keep his job,' thought Gillespie. Thomson immediately went up a couple of notches in his estimation; he was willing to put his career on the line for his subordinates. Unlike the majority of senior officers he had met, who spent most of their time picking holes in whatever was done and sloped shoulders whenever it came to taking responsibility. The nine o'clock 'shoulders' drove him crazy. If anything happened overnight the senior officers who turned up at nine o'clock in the morning would say, 'You should 'ave done this, or you should 'ave done that.' Hindsight is a wonderful thing.

Inside the house MacLeod sat in the study with Balfour. He had been told to sit in a leather-winged chair and it would be impossible for him to get up quickly to disarm Balfour. On the walls of the study was a collection of knives, swords and guns, contained in locked glass fronted cabinets. Each had a silhouette drawn around the weapon, such that if any weapon were moved it would clearly be seen which item was gone. He saw some handguns were missing. He also noticed with a start that a knife was missing, one which had an identical silhouette to the one that was now in the possession of his team, the one that had been used to cut off Campbell's head.

'I see that you have handed in some of your handguns,' said MacLeod. He deliberately did not ask about the knife, if he asked now it might push this man over the edge.

Balfour gazed absent-mindedly at the cabinet. 'Yes, I did what the law required and handed them in. I don't see what the problem is by having handguns. I'm not a nutter, I wouldn't kill anyone.'

MacLeod refrained from commenting about

the present situation; it would not help in the circumstances.

'I'm not going to hurt you, I was thinking about killing myself when that young officer came to the door. I didn't mean to frighten him, it was a mistake to have this in my hand when I told him to go away. I'm sorry about that. I should have hidden, I saw you and your side-kick earlier on and hid under the kitchen table.'

'That will teach me to be more persevering in future,' thought MacLeod. 'If we had pushed it then this may not have happened,' he said to Balfour. 'I don't think you really want to kill yourself.'

'Oh, yes I do.' Balfour gripped the shotgun and MacLeod immediately tried to calm him by saying, 'All right, you do. Why would you want to do that, think of your wife and children, how are they going to take it?'

Balfour put his head down and tears flowed from his eyes without restraint. 'My wife is dead in the bedroom. We had an argument and I hit her, she fell against the window ledge and she broke her neck. It was an accident, honestly, I didn't mean to kill her.'

MacLeod stiffened in total shock. Never had a murderer been so calm when admitting his or her actions. He said as calmly and as matter of fact as he could, 'You know I should caution you now.'

'Go ahead, take notes if you want to. It doesn't matter, you can say what you like once I'm dead.' Balfour was bitter, upset and angry. He was feeling every emotion and his system was on overload.

MacLeod took this window of opportunity to get a rapport with Balfour. 'I'll listen, maybe if you talk about it you may feel better. You know very well I will do anything I can to stop you harming yourself.'

'I know it's your job,' Balfour sneered.

'Yes, it is my job, but in your case I like you and I feel you have been pushed over the edge for some reason. I know why you want to kill yourself. A lawyer in jail has as hard a time as a police officer, but if it was an accident you may not go to prison,' said MacLeod. He leant forward in the chair and gazed into Balfour's eyes, the windows of the soul. He could read someone's intentions by looking into their eyes. In Balfour's case the windows showed eternal agony, but also the hesitation to cause his own self-destruction appeared for a fleeting moment.

'Good, he's wavering,' thought MacLeod. 'I must build on this.'

'I killed her, and I killed Campbell too.

I will go to prison.' Balfour's voice was strained.

MacLeod had had Balfour as his main suspect for some time, and his comment that he would go to prison indicated he had changed his mind about killing himself. All he had to do now was to get the gun off him to save his own skin and Balfour's. He didn't want an accident now. He decided to get Balfour thinking of something else. Once his guard was down he might be able to retrieve the gun safely.

'Mrs Campbell has admitted killing her husband. She's in intensive care at the moment, she's had a heart attack,' said MacLeod.

'No, she didn't kill him. I did. She told me about six months ago that my wife and her husband were having an affair. I had suspected it anyway, and Julia only confirmed my suspicions. It was the photograph that proved it. Fran is looking at William with such love.' He gritted his teeth. 'She was laughing at me.'

'Was that the one I saw in your office?' asked MacLeod.

'Yes, we were so happy then, I didn't put two and two together until Julia wrote me a letter telling me what was going on. I watched Fran very carefully. They were clever, I couldn't catch them. Until Saturday that is. I overheard Fran arranging a meeting at the kirk. I went there and saw them together in the car park. I saw William get out of the car and walk up to the kirk. I was crazy with jealousy and followed him. He told me there was nothing between him and Julia but I knew different and I hit him and somehow my hands were round his neck and he was dead.'

Balfour put his head in his hands and began to cry. He let go of the shotgun and MacLeod gently took it from him and, unloading it, put it on the floor. Balfour looked at MacLeod with such pain that MacLeod's heart lurched.

'Come with me,' MacLeod said as he helped Balfour to his feet. He assisted him to the door and supported him to the police car where he handed him over to Sergeant Gillespie. 'Take him to the station and have a doctor see him. I'll follow later.' Sergeant Gillespie took him away.

Thomson said to MacLeod, 'Are you OK?'

'Yes, but I'm afraid we have another body. Mrs Balfour is dead in the bedroom. I haven't seen the corpse yet, I wanted to make sure he was out of the house safely before I went back. Balfour has admitted killing both his wife and Campbell, but there are too many loose ends. I haven't asked him about Charlie Steele's murder, that can wait till later. We will have to interview him once the doctor certifies him fit.'

Thomson said to MacLeod, 'In the meantime I think we will see the Fiscal on the way back. He's got a great interest in this case. After all they were friends. He will get someone else to take over the case. It's only right and it would be better if we know now who is to take over.' Thomson turned to Detective Inspector MacBain and said, 'Get the police surgeon and forensic out here to do the necessary. Hopefully we can have a preliminary report on the cause of death before we formally interview Balfour.'

'Not another post-mortem,' said Janet, 'that will be the third one in as many days.'

MacLeod said to Janet, 'You seem to have drawn the short straw again. Never mind, I'll make it up to you, I promise, scout's honour.' He held up three fingers of his right hand in a salute.

'You were never a boy scout,' said Milton. 'The nearest you ever got was to cuddle a girl guide behind the bike sheds.'

'Wrong. I was and for your cheek you can go with her to the mortuary,' said MacLeod.

He got into the passenger seat of Thomson's car and they headed off to see the Fiscal.

As they left Janet said, 'I wonder which is going to be more scary for Mr MacLeod, the gun pointed at his head or the car ride.'

Milton observed dryly, 'It's going to be difficult to choose.'

'Ah well, let's get on with it. The sooner we do the sooner it's all over,' said Janet.

19

In the car Thomson said to MacLeod, 'If you ever do anything like that again, I personally will kill you myself. How would I explain to Morag and the girls what happened to you? You only thought of yourself and no-one else.'

MacLeod held his hand up and stopped the tirade of anger. 'Hark at who's talking. May I remind you of the time when you wandered into a house and faced a double-barrelled shotgun. You were in uniform then and you didn't do what the book said.'

'How did you know about that?' Thomson was shocked; he wasn't proud of his mistake that nearly got him killed.

'How? I was in the Close when this body came hurtling out of the window and landed in the dustbin area. It's a good job the rubbish hadn't been collected or he would have been killed. You threw him out of a third floor window,' said MacLeod.

'No I didn't throw him out of the window, it was an accident. I only went to serve a warrant on him and there he was, all five foot nine of him, wearing his string vest and socks, nothing else with a shotgun pointed at me. He hadn't had a shave in days. The shotgun wasn't loaded but how was I to know that. Adrenaline took over and I got mad. I didn't know the window was open, I grabbed the gun and pushed it away with my left hand. I gave him such a smack with my right, he tumbled over the settee and whoops, before I knew where I was he flipped out of the open window. I tried to stop him but it was too late. His missus came out and saw what was happening. She was a great help! 'Let the silly sod go, he's more use to me dead than alive.' I prayed he would be all right and he was, just a broken arm and a few bruises.'

As they turned left into the main road from Kilmun to Dunoon, a car shot out in front of them from the petrol station at the junction. MacLeod had seen the car move off from the petrol pumps but Thomson had not, he was too busy thinking about other things than his driving, and there was nearly a collision. MacLeod cringed in his seat, but had the sense not to say anything. 'Stupid fool,' shouted Thomson and continued careering on his way. MacLeod was relieved to get to the Dunoon's Office in George Street in one piece.

They went into the reception. Mrs Stewart

seemed subdued. When she saw them she said, 'Mr Grey is waiting for you, we had a call to say that you were on your way. He knows what happened at Mr Balfour's house.' She took them straight into the Fiscal's office.

'Sergeant Gillespie rang me and told me briefly what happened; I can't believe it. Is it true that James Balfour held you hostage, Cameron?' said the Fiscal.

'Yes and no, Balfour is in a state of shock, he wanted to kill himself, not me. I went in willingly and I was never in any danger.' MacLeod was certain of this fact.

'You shouldn't have done it; anyone brandishing a gun is dangerous and I think it might have been better if the armed officers had dealt with it,' said Grey.

'If that had happened he may have been killed, he was pointing a gun and you know what armed officers would do, they would have taken him out. Or is that better than what is going to happen now? It would have saved a trial and dirty washing being aired in public,' retorted MacLeod.

'You know better than that, Mr MacLeod.' Grey became formal. 'Balfour is a friend and I don't believe in trial by gun.'

'I'm sorry, I didn't mean it, I'm still in shock you know.'

'That's all right, Cameron, I'll make allowances for you if you will for me.' Grey was showing how distressed he was. He had felt from the beginning that this murder would cause deep distress to everyone connected to it, and he was no exception.

Grey turned to Thomson. 'What is it I can do for you?'

'First could you tell me if Mrs Julia Campbell has come to your notice in an official capacity. It's been alleged that she was a nasty vindictive woman who had no compunction in writing untrue allegations in letters to her neighbours and treating anyone she did not regard as her equal like muck.' MacLeod did not pull his punches.

Grey was startled. 'I've never heard of anything like that, not in all the time I have known her. Wait a minute, someone did tell Maureen, that she was a bad neighbour and no-one would speak to her. I put that down to jealousy and didn't take much notice, but that was years ago. Julia told me that the neighbours in question were making life hell for her, throwing things in her garden, noisy parties and the like. Julia is a nice person and I can't imagine her doing anything like that.'

'I'm afraid she isn't what she seems; she did tell James Balfour that his wife was having an affair with William Campbell and the proof was in your house,' said MacLeod.

'Not that photo. We were all laughing at something. William had said something and we were all looking at him. It was taken by the chalet maid for us; if it had been taken a moment later I expect Fran Balfour would have been looking at me. Have you asked Fran about it?' queried Grey.

'I thought Sergeant Gillespie told you what happened at the Balfour home?' said Thomson. Realisation dawned on him that Grey did not know that Fran Balfour was dead and that Balfour had admitted killing her.

'He did. Cameron talked James out of killing himself and brought him out with no harm done. What else is there?' asked Grey.

MacLeod said to Thomson, 'Sergeant Gillespie left before I told you what had happened in the house, so he didn't know the rest and couldn't have told the Fiscal everything. Do you want to tell him or shall I?'

Thomson said, 'You do it, you know more than I do.'

Turning to Grey, MacLeod said, 'I'm very sorry to tell you this but James Balfour murdered his wife as well as his friend William Campbell. I expect he also murdered Charlie Steele, though I haven't put that to him yet.'

Grey looked as if he had been shot. He sat back in his chair with a thump. 'I suspected he had killed William, that would be the only reason for his stupid actions but not Fran, I thought she was at her mother's.'

'We all did, but I was suspicious when he wouldn't let us see her. I thought she had left him, not been murdered. In fact we were going to try to see her today when all this blew up,' said MacLeod.

'Well, I'd better hand this over to my deputy, I'm too closely involved. Her name is Janice Smith, she's a very capable lawyer, she'll go far if she puts her mind to it. Janice is out at the moment; I'll get her to contact you when she gets back. Meanwhile if there is anything I can do, don't hesitate to ask,' said Grey.

MacLeod said, 'Julia Campbell is in hospital, she's had a heart attack.' Before MacLeod could go any further Grey said, 'I suppose she forgot to take her pills due to the shock of her husband's death. She suffers from angina and if she forgets to take her pills for 24 hours she has a bad time. She's done it before.' He looked at MacLeod: 'Or do you believe she forgot her pills on purpose?'

'No normal person dices with their health like that,' said MacLeod. Privately he thought that if this woman was everything that had been said about her, she would use her illness as a shield to escape the consequences of her own actions. Mrs Campbell seemed to gain pleasure from the emotional pain of others and when they retaliated she could justify her own actions, always conveniently forgetting how the argument started. MacLeod had met her type before; it wasn't a pleasant experience.

They left Grey sitting in his office with the air of a man who had a great deal to think about. His private life had now been defiled by these shocking events. A murder is never only an act of violence on the victim; the ripples are felt throughout the family, friends and even acquaintances. Anyone touched by the ultimate evil is changed forever. Police officers dealing with the crime do not escape the trauma either.

Back at the police office, MacLeod decided to see the two boys, Ewen Jones and Iain Campbell. They had been held in custody whilst investigations had continued. He felt that keeping them in custody further would not serve the interests of justice, and as soon as he could he would release them. He told

Detective Sergeant Susan Lampart to sit in with him. The rest of the team was busy in the routine matters relating to the death of Mrs Balfour: identification, forensic and witness statements. Just because someone admits to something, it doesn't stop the collection of evidence. It has been known that false confessions have been made, but very unlikely in this case. Susan was lucky because she was with MacLeod; she had missed the third post-mortem, for this she was extremely grateful and felt heartily sorry for Detective Inspector Janet MacBain.

MacLeod had the opportunity to go and see James Balfour as the doctor had certified him as fit, but MacLeod wanted the preliminary results of Mrs Balfour's post-mortem before he did so. He preferred to have all the facts when conducting an important interview. It also allowed Balfour time to think.

Ewen was first. MacLeod showed him the haversack that had recently contained the head of William Campbell. 'Is this yours?' he asked. 'Yes,' said Ewen, 'and I did put the head in it. I saw Iain in Glasgow; he was really upset and told me that his mum had rung him last week. She had said that his dad had been having lots of affairs and she was going to do something about it once and for all. Well it preyed on his mind and

273

he took off from the digs and came home.'

'When was this?' asked MacLeod.

'Oh, last Saturday. When I found out I followed him. I knew that his dad would be in the kirk so I went straight there and saw Iain. He was wild; his dad was dead and he was hacking at his neck with a knife. I only arrived after it was all over. He stabbed his dad with that knife, we tried to get it out but couldn't, so I wiped the knife clean of any fingerprints and after sneaking into my home, got the haversack and hid the head — under the stairs at first, then I put it in the old ruin after it had been searched by you lot.'

'Why did you try and hide it?' MacLeod was intrigued.

'I hoped someone would think it was a madman that had killed him and Iain wouldn't be suspected,' replied Ewen. 'Iain wanted to hang it up over the kirk to show his father was a traitor to his mother. I thought that was just too horrible for words.'

'When did you find out that Mr Campbell was already dead when Iain got to the kirk?' asked MacLeod.

'When we got into town, it took me a long time to get Iain calmed down. I decided it would be a good idea to get arrested so we could have an alibi, and Iain went along with everything I said. It's my fault, I should have called the police when I found him dead. I'm so very sorry.' Ewen seemed genuinely upset at his actions. 'Have you told my Mum yet?'

'No. I think you should do that, but if you need some support with her Detective Sergeant Lampart will go with you.'

'Yes please.' He needed help and knew it.

'I expect your career in Law has been severely curtailed. The University may take a dim view of you trying to conceal a very serious crime.'

The subsequent interview with young Iain Campbell was short and brief. In fact it was more of a monologue than an interview. Iain started talking as soon as MacLeod came into the room. MacLeod had to stop him talking while they set up the tape recorder. Once the warning bleep had subsided MacLeod only managed to say, 'I remind you that you are under caution', when he was interrupted.

Iain said, 'Yes, I know. I didn't kill my father but I cut off his head. Ewen shouldn't have stopped me putting it on a pole to show everyone he took after the 'Traitor Campbell'. Then when Ewen took me away I realised what I had done and everything else is a haze. I did what Ewen said. I'm sorry, but Mum's been so good and Dad was so awful to her.'

MacLeod interrupted the torrent of words to ask the question to which he needed an answer. 'Where did you get the knife?'

'I found it on the path up to the kirk, someone must have dropped it. I felt it was God's will to give me the tools for the job,' replied Iain.

MacLeod noted that his eyes had an unnatural gleam and the young man's hands were shaking. He told Susan to wait with him and left the room. 'Gillespie, get hold of a doctor, that young man is slipping over the edge to insanity. I want him seen as soon as possible and he is not to be left alone at any time. If he gets really agitated put Ewen Jones in with him. I think his friend may be able to help.'

Sergeant Gillespie groaned. How many nutters could they cope with? He just didn't have an unlimited supply of officers to do everything. They had the area to police still; just because a couple of murders had been committed it didn't stop his other duties. He didn't grumble out loud, but got on with it as usual.

MacLeod said to Susan, 'This boy is your responsibility from now until he is let out of the station. He'll probably be going to hospital, but whatever happens look after him.'

The phone rang. Gillespie answered it and said to MacLeod, 'It's for you, Detective Inspector MacBain.'

The conversation was brief. MacLeod was given a preliminary report on Fran Balfour's post-mortem. The estimated time of death was consistent with everything James Balfour had said. The cause of death was crushing blows to the head.

20

Detective Superintendent Thomson decided to accompany MacLeod when he interviewed James Balfour. The bottom line was that he was nosy. As the officer in charge of the investigation, it was his prerogative to conduct the interview but he felt that he didn't have enough information to talk properly to Balfour, nor did he have MacLeod's obvious rapport with him; therefore he told MacLeod that he should get on with it.

James Balfour was slumped in the chair in interview room one where Iain Campbell had so recently sat. MacLeod recognised the same spark of insanity in Balfour as he had seen in young Iain. Iain's young mind could not cope with it, Balfour on the other hand was just hanging on. Tea in one of those disgusting polystyrene cups was slowly congealing in front of him. There was an unnatural air of calm about Balfour that concerned MacLeod; it was a prelude to something else.

MacLeod switched on the tape recorder and the high-pitched whine reverberated round the room, bouncing from wall to wall and stirring Balfour from his lethargy. MacLeod formally introduced both himself and Detective Superintendent Thomson.

Balfour looked at MacLeod with hollow deadened eyes and said, 'I'm a lawyer remember, I know what this is all about. I've been to hell and back since Saturday. I don't know what came over me, it was a kind of madness I suppose. You must understand I'm not really a violent man, it was as if I was watching myself do these things. I wish you had let me die.'

MacLeod was affronted. 'I'm not in the game of letting people die, I've taken an oath to protect life. Yours is as precious as any one else's no matter what you have done.'

Thomson was getting irritated at this cosy scene. He was restless and shuffled in his seat. Balfour was a murderer and in his book had forfeited the right to live by taking another's life. MacLeod on the other hand saw a difference between a cold-blooded murderer who killed for the pleasure of the act and this pathetic apology for a human being sitting in front of him. This man had allowed his jealousy to take hold of his life and thus killed what he most loved, his wife and his best friend. Balfour could only be treated with sympathy or he would clam up and MacLeod would never find out what really happened.

'What on earth made you do it?' MacLeod asked.

'I don't know why I snapped, Julia had told me about the affair, and she rang on Saturday to tip me off; I had to know. Fran went out about eight o'clock, it was just getting dark. I knew she would be going to the kirk to see William so I decided to follow her. I drove to the car park at Benmore Gardens; you can see everything from there. I saw William get into the car. I was raging, I waited and waited and she left about an hour later. I knew they had been having sex. The windows were steamed up. When he left he kissed her on the cheek.'

Balfour's face was contorted with the kind of anger and grief that both MacLeod and Thomson hoped they would never experience. Balfour continued: 'I climbed the wall of the graveyard and followed him into the kirk. He actually smiled, he had been with my wife and he smiled at me. It was too much. He wanted me to pray with him after just making love to my wife. I hit him with the first thing that came to hand. It was a heavy candlestick. I tried to clean it up and put it back on the altar. Then I strangled him with my bare hands.' He put his head in his hands.

'How did the body get to the gravestone?' asked Thomson.

'I carried him most of the way. Don't ask me where I got the strength from, I suppose it was the strength of a madman. I wanted everyone to see him when they came to morning prayer. So stupid, I don't know what came over me. I was quite proud of what I had done.' He paused and said with resigned emphasis, 'Then.'

MacLeod brought the knife into Balfour's line of sight, 'Is this yours?'

Balfour looked at it. 'Yes, I got it in Malaya when I was in the Army. One of the Aussies gave me it as a souvenir, I was quite proud of it. No-one round here had one and it was a talking point at dinner parties. I took it with me. I'm surprised the Fiscal didn't remember it, but we were always drunk when I brought it out. I didn't know what I was going to do with it, perhaps stab him? I don't know. I must have dropped it somewhere because I didn't have it when I got home.'

'What happened next?' asked MacLeod. This was not an interview it was more of a conversation. Balfour seemed to be using this time as a confessional. 'I got home and confronted Fran. I told her I had killed her lover and she got hysterical. She told me that she had only gone to see William to get him to see me and talk to me. Me? There's nothing wrong with me. She said I had changed over the last six months and she wanted me to get back to normal. I ask you how could I get back to normal when she had William as a lover. She then said she was going to call the police. I wanted to reason with her but she wouldn't listen, so I hit her. She hit her head on the window ledge and she was dead.'

MacLeod had received the preliminary report from the pathologist. Fran had been hit with a blunt instrument on at least twenty occasions. He decided not to challenge whatever version Balfour cared to give on this particular murder unless he denied actually touching her. No amount of questioning would move Balfour's mind into accepting that he had bludgeoned his wife so brutally; that would be for the courts to decide. This was another fact that he would keep from Balfour. Fran had not had sexual intercourse for at least two weeks before her death and was not the woman William Campbell had been with that night. Neither Thomson nor MacLeod wished to push him completely over the edge.

'What happened to Charlie Steele?' asked MacLeod quietly.

'I killed him. You see he rang me, he told me that he had seen me going into the kirk that night and wanted money. I had just killed my wife and my best friend, it seemed easier to get rid of him too. I was sad I had to do it, I liked Charlie and he really didn't deserve to die, but he had to. You understand?' Balfour looked at Thomson and MacLeod in turn, his eyes pleading for understanding. Neither man did understand but nodded to encourage him along and obtain what evidence they needed.

'I arranged to meet him at Jubilee Point at Loch Eck. I knew that if I could kill him and push both him and his car into the Loch it would not be found. The Loch is very deep; I fish it regularly and know it like the back of my hand. That was the only murder that I really thought about. The other two, well, they really were on the spur of the moment.' This estimation of the crimes was at variance with MacLeod's thinking; he had believed that William Campbell's murder was pre-meditated. The other two were spur of the moment, but no matter, it would all sort itself out later.

Some fifteen minutes later after James Balfour had been placed in the cells Thomson and MacLeod were sitting in the office carefully going over the 'conversation' they had had with Balfour. 'Do you believe him?' asked Thomson.

'Yes, I do. He is a weak man and has been manipulated into doing this thing.'

'By whom, may I ask?' Thomson was intrigued.

MacLeod replied, 'By Mrs Campbell of course. I could never prove it, but I believe that she has been trying for years to get her husband out of the way. She's been prodding neighbours by writing untruths to them about their wives and that included her own daughters. Fortunately the ones she has wrongly accused in the past had a good open relationship with their husbands and they talked about it. James Balfour was a jealous man who actually believed these accusations. She stirred him up for months until he didn't know what he was doing.'

'Don't be silly, she couldn't do that; she may have wanted her husband beaten up, but not murdered. How could she know James would kill?'

'She didn't but she hoped it would happen. I think she has wanted him dead for years. I think she knew that James was going to do something serious that night, after all she stripped her husband's bed after he had gone out. She knew he wasn't coming back.'

It was Thomson's turn to be surprised, 'Stripped his bed!'

'Yes, Detective Sergeant Lampart looked at the house again. The only room not packed was hers. She knew she wouldn't be moving the following day. William's bedroom was completely stripped of bedclothes; she did that on the Saturday night after he went out. I checked with WPC O'Neill who said that the only time Mrs Campbell went upstairs was to bed to sleep. She looked round the house then and saw that William Campbell's bedroom was exactly as Detective Sergeant Lampart had seen it. Therefore she didn't expect him home.'

'Nice logic, but how do you prove that Julia Campbell is behind all this?' asked Thomson.

'We can't prove it, and I would never try. It would be laughed out of court if it ever got that far. You know the worst thing about it all. She actually accused her daughters of having sex with their own father, knowing it was a lie. She tried to stir up one of her sons-in-law to violence. Fortunately her girls knew their mother well and kept their families away from the house.' MacLeod could not imagine a worse crime than incest and to accuse an innocent, loving father was the height of depravity.

Sergeant Gillespie came into the room and said, 'A lady is downstairs and wants to see someone in charge of the murder case. She won't give me her name and I would like to keep it that way.'

'You mean you know her?' said MacLeod.

'Perhaps, but if she won't tell me who she is I don't know, now do I?' Gillespie replied.

MacLeod went into the sergeant's office where he saw a handsome woman of indeterminate age; she was well dressed and seemed nervous. He introduced himself and she launched into an obviously rehearsed speech.

'I was having an affair with William Campbell; he was with me on the Saturday evening at my home. I dropped him off near the kirk about eight fifteen. I've been a widow for three years now, he was good company at first and things just developed.' Beginning to shake, she paused to take a clean pristine white handkerchief out of her handbag and dab her eyes. She visibly controlled herself, and went on to say, 'We were going to live together eventually. I should have come to you sooner but it's taken me some courage to come now. I don't want my name brought into it.' She looked pleadingly at MacLeod.

'I think we can keep your name out of it,

you haven't told us who you are anyway but if the Fiscal wants to know then I'm sure we could trace you. Thank you for coming in.'

She smiled at MacLeod as he escorted her out of the building. When he came back he said to Gillespie, 'Out of curiosity, who was that?'

'It's Mrs Edgar, she lives not far from the kirk in Kilmun. She probably won't remember me, I had to give her the news that her husband had been killed on the oil rigs some years ago. A sad case; they couldn't have children and she's alone in the world. I like her and if she and the Reverend got together it's none of my business.'

'Quite right,' said MacLeod. 'That's one problem solved, and I expect it was true that Fran Balfour only went to see Campbell because her husband was acting crazy over the last few months. She wanted a friend to talk to and who better then the local minister and her husband's best friend? So the semen found by Alisdair was nothing to do with this case. Obviously some courting couple had found the place open and used it. The activities of the police over the last few days would make the kirk grounds out of bounds for that sort of thing, until the excitement died down and life returned to normal.' MacLeod was unsure when that would be. Sometimes what seems to be a relevant clue to an investigation turns out to be a red herring. The use of the small hut was just one of those times.

Thomson returned to his desk at Force HQ, and MacLeod and his team were left to clear up the paper work.

James Balfour and Iain Campbell were both examined by Doctor Moorbath and he admitted them immediately to Lochgilphead mental hospital for observations. He was worried about the visible deterioration in their mental health as they began to realise what they had done. He told MacLeod that he had hoped that Iain would make a full recovery. He had no such hope for James whom he believed would probably spend the rest of his life in hospital — if he didn't kill himself of course: he would have to be on suicide watch for some time.

Ewen Jones was allowed bail into the care of his mother. It seemed that all the loose ends were being sorted out.

Whilst they were clearing up, Detective Constable Morris failed to notice that Susan Lampart had slipped out and was organising an impromptu party at the Argyll Hotel in Dunoon to celebrate his marriage. The team was not to be denied. Mrs White was delighted to help and made a private room available for them. She quickly got a buffet together and decided that even if this was the busy period and they were almost full, she would keep the few vacant rooms left for the remnants of the party. She had some experience of police parties, the 'left-overs' were usually too drunk to move, never mind get home!

MacLeod had a bee in his bonnet about Julia Campbell; he couldn't let it rest and had a long discussion with the deputy Fiscal, although she agreed with him — there was no evidence to support any charge.

MacLeod went to the hospital on his way to the Argyll hotel, on the off chance he could see Julia Campbell. She was sitting in a chair beside her bed like a queen bee, with no sign of the distress she had shown the previous times he had been with her. She looked at him with a steady gaze. 'Worked it out then, Mister MacLeod?' She emphasised the Mister. 'I thought you would, no fool our Mister MacLeod.'

MacLeod bristled with hardly concealed fury. This woman used words as a weapon and she was getting to him. Keeping his temper he calmly said, 'Yes. Did you expect your husband to be killed?'

Julia looked round. 'As it's you and me I'll tell you. No I didn't, it was a bonus. I expected him to be beaten up and end up in hospital for a few weeks. I hoped that he would be so badly injured and he would be reliant on me. You know he's had a few 'accidents' over the years. But someone was looking after him. The worst he got was a sprained ankle.'

MacLeod said, 'So you tried to kill him?'

Julia looked quite genuinely shocked. 'No, I wouldn't do that. Anyway, if a husband dies at home the first person you suspect is the wife. I wouldn't have been able to get away with it. It was much better this way.'

'Why didn't you get a divorce? It would have been easier than all of this,' said MacLeod.

'Oh no it wouldn't, divorce is not in my vocabulary. I had him well insured, not too much to make it suspicious, but enough. I spent my whole life serving him and his brats. I wanted a life of my own. He wouldn't even sleep with me, I was his housekeeper and that was all I was to him. I've shown him, haven't I? He was having an affair with that slut Fran Balfour.'

MacLeod was shocked at the callous person sitting before him. She had engineered the death of her husband and she had no obvious remorse for the results of her actions. MacLeod was not a man who usually reacted to provocation, but he felt like it and allowed himself the luxury of wiping the smile off this woman's face.

'He wasn't having an affair with Fran Balfour but with someone a lot younger and more attractive, someone also free to go with him.' He allowed this to sink in before he continued. 'Your friend James Balfour is in the mental hospital and will probably never be able to stand trial, your son is in the same hospital having hacked the head off your husband. Your three daughters are never going to speak to you again and your neighbours are going to have a 'Hurrah She's Gone' party. So who's won now? Enjoy your lonely victory. If I ever get enough evidence to charge you, I will and I won't stop looking.'

Turning on his heel he left, missing the mask of hate that swept over Julia Campbell's face, but he felt her eyes boring into him.

MacLeod felt a little better. He knew he had almost succeeded in blackmailing her to leave the area and start a new life elsewhere. He was not proud of his actions, but somehow he had a sense of achievement. 'God help the place she goes to,' he thought. 'At least she will be out of my hair.'

As he went through the door he suddenly

remembered a detail, something unimportant to anyone but himself. He turned and stared into Julia's face; she had managed to control her emotions and was, to all appearances, cool, calm and collected.

'Yes,' she said. 'Can't leave me alone?' The words were outwardly innocuous, but he heard an implied sexual connotation. He mentally slapped himself. This woman was capable of anything; why had he seen her alone? He had foolishly left himself open to allegations and shuddered at the thought.

He opened the door wider and did not walk back into the room. Fortunately she was in a hospital with many staff within hearing distance. She could never accuse him of improper behaviour, nevertheless he was extremely wary.

'One thing,' MacLeod said, 'what happened to your copy of the photograph of your holiday in Switzerland?'

Julia cocked her head to one side. 'You mean the one I waved under James Balfour's nose and persuaded him that Fran was having an affair with William?' she asked.

'Yes, that one.'

She laughed. 'I buried it of course, like I buried three of the people in it. Give me time, I'll bury the other two as well.' Her laugh was one of triumph.

MacLeod was shaken to the core, and said, 'Are you threatening Mr and Mrs Grey?'

Julia stopped laughing and said, 'Don't be silly. I would never do that to my friends. They are older than I am, which means that I will outlive them.' Her eyes glittered.

MacLeod left. He did not know what to do which was unusual for him. He thought about telling Duncan Grey at once, but he had no proof of her threat. What she had said was reasonable and explainable, but he knew that tone of voice meant something else. No, he would sleep on it. Morag always listened when he had a particularly hard decision to make and talking to her cleared his head. He thanked God he had married her and not someone like the harridan he had just left.

★ ★ ★

MacLeod was driving away from the hospital and was about to turn down Queen's Street when he suddenly remembered young Morris's party. He couldn't go home without showing his face. He would have just one drink then leave. Parties always went better after the boss left.

When MacLeod arrived at the party, Morris was standing in the middle of the room. His face was flushed, it only needed one drink to bring the redness to his face, and he was surrounded by the rest of the team. Peter Reade was in the process of toasting his health. MacLeod stood in the doorway for a few seconds; he was sloughing the evil he had left, in the guise of Julia Campbell, and allowing the clean atmosphere of this celebration into his soul.

Milton noticed him and handed him a glass of his favourite whiskey, 'Here,' he said quietly, 'wipe it out of your mind.'

MacLeod smiled, Milton knew him so well, too well sometimes. 'Right, finished the toast have you Peter? I have one of my own, 'To the best team of detectives I have ever had the privilege to work with.' He raised his glass and ignored the incredulous looks from them all. It was the first time he had said such a thing. It would probably be the last time too.

We do hope that you have enjoyed reading this large print book.

Did you know that all of our titles are available for purchase?

We publish a wide range of high quality large print books including:
Romances, Mysteries, Classics
General Fiction
Non Fiction and Westerns

Special interest titles available in large print are:
The Little Oxford Dictionary
Music Book
Song Book
Hymn Book
Service Book

Also available from us courtesy of Oxford University Press:
Young Readers' Dictionary
(large print edition)
Young Readers' Thesaurus
(large print edition)

For further information or a free brochure, please contact us at:
Ulverscroft Large Print Books Ltd.,
The Green, Bradgate Road, Anstey,
Leicester, LE7 7FU, England.
Tel: (00 44) **0116 236 4325**
Fax: (00 44) **0116 234 0205**

BLOOD PROOF

Bill Knox

Colin Thane of the elite Scottish Crime Squad is sent north from Glasgow to the Scottish Highlands after a vicious arson attack at Broch Distillery has left three men dead and eight million pounds worth of prime stock destroyed. Finn Rankin, who runs the distillery with the aid of his three daughters, is at first unhelpful, then events take a dramatic turn for the worse. To uncover the truth, Thane must head back to Glasgow and its underworld, with one more race back to the mountains needed before the terror can finally be ended.

ISLAND OF FLOWERS

Jean M. Long

'Swallowfield' had belonged to Bethany Tyler's family for generations, but now Aunt Sophie, who lived on Jersey, was claiming her share of the property. It seemed that the only way of raising the capital was to sell the house, but then, unexpectedly, Justin Rochel arrived in Sussex and things took on a new dimension. Bethany accompanied her father and sister to Jersey, where there were shocks in store for her. She was attracted to Justin, but could she trust him?

BIRD

Jane Adams

Marcie has come to the bedside of her dying grandfather to make her peace. For Jack Whitney was the man who raised her, who loved her as if she was his own daughter, and from whom she ran away when she was just sixteen . . . But Jack is haunted by the terrible vision of a body hanging from a tree and the ghostly image of 'Rebekkah', a woman he insists is standing beside him, a noose around her neck. Marcie vows to uncover the true story behind this woman — even if it points to her grandfather being a murderer . . .